I0772777

THE HOUSEWIFE ASSASSIN'S UNDERWATER ASSETS

The Housewife Assassin Series
Book 24

JOSIE BROWN

A BOOK BY

SIGNAL
PRESS

ONE OF MANY GREAT SIGNAL PRESS BOOKS

San Francisco, CA

This is a work of fiction. All incidents and dialogue, and all characters with the exception of some well-known historical and public figures, are products of the author's imagination and are not to be construed as real.

Library of Congress Cataloging-in-Publication Data is available upon request

Cover Design/Book Conversion by Austin Brown

Trade Paperback ISBN: 978-1-970093-43-8

Hardcover ISBN: 978-1-970093-33-9

V053024

Praise for Josie Brown's Novels

"The last book that made me laugh: *The Housewife Assassin's Handbook*. Brown's unorthodox surprises did make me laugh. I taught it in a class about comic novels."
Jane Smiley, Pulitzer Prize-Winning Author

"This book hits all the right notes...I now want a week at the beach to read them all...I'm completely smitten."
Barbara Vey

"On many days, I'll join deep discussions about the works of Le Carré, Deighton, Greene, Ambler, and Forsyth. And then I take incredible delight in a series like *The Housewife Assassin*. Just the name would likely cause eyebrows to be raised, and likely, my stature as an 'expert' falls a bit. Too bad! I read for enjoyment. The authors mentioned above all entertained the heck out of me. And so does Josie Brown's wonderfully fun and amusing series about Donna Stone."
Randall Masteller, *Spy Guys + Gals*

"Brown writes the kind of feminist action plot that men should be reading, especially male authors, to cure that trope of 'vapid sexy girl with a gun.' There's enough comedy sprinkled in between the emotional scenes and within the action to keep readers' minds from going too grim here. As for the sex scenes, these are the best I've ever read. No airy poetry and metaphors. Brown accomplishes setting the mood whether Donna is willing and able or whenever Donna isn't sure what she wants. Brown's hired gun plot is fun, sometimes aggravating, and filled with the wonderful twist of being from a mother's POV."

Amber Love

Novels in The Housewife Assassin Series

The Housewife Assassin's Tips for

Weddings, Weapons, and Warfare

(Book 11)

The Housewife Assassin's Husband Hunting Hints

(Book 12)

The Housewife Assassin's Ghost Protocol

(Book 13)

The Housewife Assassin's Terrorist TV Guide

(Book 14)

The Housewife Assassin's Deadly Dossier

(Book 15: The Series Prequel)

The Housewife Assassin's Greatest Hits

(Book 16)

The Housewife Assassin's Fourth Estate Sale

(Book 17)

The Housewife Assassin's Horrorscope

(Book 18)

The Housewife Assassin's White House Keeping Seal of Approval

(Book 19)

The Housewife Assassin's Assassination Vacation Planner

(Book 20)

The Housewife Assassin's Antisocial Media Tips

(Book 21)

The Housewife Assassin's Manners,

Missiles, and Mayhem

(Book 22)

The Housewife Assassin's Gambit

(Book 23)

The Housewife Assassin's Underwater Assets

(Book 24)

Underwater Asset

An "underwater asset" is a financial instrument currently worth less than you paid for it.

For example, homeowners are considered "underwater" if their mortgage is larger than their home's current value.

The same can be said about relationships. An emotional foreclosure may be imminent if you or your partner value each other less than when you first fell in love.

In marital terms, this is known as a "divorce."

Solution: A continuous investment of time, effort, communication, and sex will undoubtedly bring it out of the red and perhaps make it your most precious asset.

Time to find out, wouldn't you say?

The palm trees surrounding our lagoon's sugary beach sway gently like drunken dancers at last call. The ocean breezes counterbalance the hot sun in the cloudless sky. If you've deduced that my husband Jack and I are far away from the rest of humanity (not to mention our stock in trade: avenging the horrendous crimes against it), you'd be spot on.

We are at Kisiwa Cha Paradiso, a private island off the coast of Zanzibar that can accommodate only thirty guests at a time.

When we checked in last week, our personal concierge, Tisa, took us by golf cart to our cabana on a private inlet named Happy Parrot Lagoon. Though this glass mega-hut looks rustic on the outside, its interior is tricked out with all the amenities that encourage pleasure and pampering: a two-person tub surrounded by an abundant collection of scented candles and lots of bubbles and bath salts, a fireplace, lazily whirling ceiling fans, a fully stocked gourmet galley kitchen, and a small wine cellar.

To the rich, the celebrated, or the infamous, even Kisiwa Cha Paradiso's plethora of luxuries takes second place to its promise of absolute privacy. Guests expect to be unplugged and off the grid: no cell phones, WiFi, internet connection, computers, television, or satellite phone. The postman doesn't ring at all, let alone twice.

Arrivals and departures—via yacht or plane—are scheduled in advance and are strictly adhered to, unless there's an emergency. Or, to quote its brochure: "Though rare, here at Kisiwa Cha Paradiso, any unforeseen incidents that may cause a guest's change of plans is regrettable, but accommodated with speed and discretion."

After reading this, Jack declared, "With all this

luxury, who'd ever want to leave? Heck, I want to move in permanently!"

But of course, he does. I can't say I blame him.

Our personal concierge, Tisa, assured us, "If it is your desire, you never have to see anyone else—guest or staff."

After placing leis around our necks, she handed me a turquoise electronic pad. DONNA AND JACK were inscribed on it. With a dimpled smile, she added, "However, should you need anything at all, just write it here"— she opened the screen, which showed an electronic note-card embellished with parrots—"and tap to send. You'll hear a bell when I leave the requested item in your hut's dumbwaiter."

As she pointed to the built-in drawer, an ornate bracelet glistened on her wrist: sterling silver, adorned with her name.

"How beautiful!" I exclaimed.

"A gift from someone dear to me: my brother." When she smiled, her dimples deepened. "Now, one last thing before I go!" She then offered to take our picture with the electronic pad.

The next day, the photo was delivered in a frame crafted from island shells. In it, we are out on the terrace with our private lagoon as the backdrop. Jack has his arms around me and is kissing my neck.

Tisa was right. We haven't seen her since, nor anyone else.

That's fine with us. Instead, we've spent most of our time in the hut's centerpiece: a king-size bed.

There, we make love: gently at first. Until our passion

gets the better of us. Our orgasms are accompanied by ecstatic moans that startle the parrots roosting in the neighboring palms. Screeching indignantly, they fly away.

Ah, well. Too bad! This much-needed vacation has been like a second honeymoon.

In truth, it's our first since the original was interrupted by Jack's kidnapping.

Between blissful bouts of lovemaking, we order room service: fish caught straight from the ocean before being spiced, grilled, and served with rice from local paddies; pineapples, mangoes, passionfruit, papaya, and bananas plucked from the surrounding trees. Other epicurean delights are created from the provisions carefully chosen by a world-renowned chef and served with appropriate wines.

Though we see no one, our every whim is sated. We know when our requests arrive because, as Tisa promised, we hear a tinkling bell as a large basket is placed in the hut's dumbwaiter.

Most importantly, we sleep as if we didn't have a care in the world.

Except for last night. For some reason, I woke up with a start. I dreamt of a loud crash.

Naked, I rolled out of bed to take a look from the floor-to-ceiling glass wall that gives us a straight-on view of our inlet. Without moonlight, all I saw was inky darkness. But my ears picked up the sound of a boat's engine, by then it had grown fainter—

Then silence.

Good. It went away.

Good riddance and bon voyage, lost yacht.

Now that we're in the middle of our second week here, we're curious enough to wander beyond the lagoon's perimeter. Jack suggests we take the trail to its tiki-adorned guest lounge.

We first pass its all-glass exercise cabana. Despite being alone, the resort's yoga instructor, lithe and muscular, is putting herself through the paces of her regimen. After positioning herself in the child's pose and then the happy baby, she moves back and forth from cat to cow to cobra before bending into a chair and, finally, the downward dog.

By the time she's shifted from the warrior to the posterior-tightening bridge lift, Jack is mesmerized.

To pull him out of his trance, I snap my fingers in his awed face. "I know those moves, too."

He smiles. "You taught me a few of them this morning."

I shake my head. "Silly boy! The Kama Sutra isn't anywhere near as relaxing."

He sighs at the memory. "But it's a helluva workout."

We go to the terrace, where a buxom barmaid is drying glasses. A brawny, bronzed bartender tosses a cocktail shaker high, catches it behind his back, and pours circular ice cubes and an amber liquid into two cut-crystal lowballs. Garnishing each glass with an orange peel, he grins at me.

Jack and I take a couple of barstools directly in front of him. "I'll bet those have our names on them," Jack declares.

"They do indeed, sir." The bartender gives me a sly

wink. "Negronis." Glancing at the clock on the wall, he adds, "In fact, you're right on time."

The barmaid giggles.

"What's so funny?" I ask.

Shyly, she ducks her head.

"What is your name?" Jack asks.

"Zahara Japhet," she says.

"And his?"

"Emmanuel Zuberi," She looks over at the bartender, who shrugs.

Jack hands her a twenty-dollar bill. "Zahara, tell us why you laughed, and you'll earn another."

She eyes the bartender.

He sighs. "You know the rules. Whatever sir and madame wish."

"But…that is even more than the staff bet…" Realizing her faux pas, her voice trails off, and her cheeks pinken. Lowering her eyes, she whispers, "Emmanuel won a bet."

Now it's Jack's turn to laugh. "Congratulations, Emmanuel! What gave us away?"

I can't stand it any longer. "What exactly are we talking about?"

My question has the barmaid giggling, whereas Emmanuel, embarrassed, rolls his eyes.

"They were betting how long before we'd come up for air," Jack explains.

Now I'm giggling, too. Finally, I gasp: "Congratulations, Emmanuel, for your lucky guess!"

"That is because he wears his lucky shoes," Zahara insists.

I hike up over the bar so I can see for myself:

She's right. I know the brand well. Not only are they lucky, but they're casual too—not to mention very expensive John Lobb loafers. Almost a thousand dollars worth, not including the shiny penny tucked into each leather band.

When I look up, I see that her remark has annoyed him. To get the mood back to mellow, I say, "You also have great taste, sir."

Stoically, he shakes his head. "It wasn't luck, madame, but an educated supposition!"

"Ah! Well, tell me how you reached your hypothesis."

"Your cabana is in Happy Parrot Lagoon," Emmanuel explains. "It's been several hours since the parrots have been scared away. I take it they must be happy again."

Jack and I laugh so hard that we almost fall off our barstools. "And how did you know we like Negronis?" I ask.

"It's my job to know, madame—and the rest of the staff is also attuned to your preferences."

"Then Tisa has done everything she promised," Jack replies. "Where is she now? I want to thank her personally."

The bartender's grin fades, and his eyes go blank. "I…was told that she has left the island."

"We're sorry to hear that," Jack replies. "I assumed she'd be here throughout our stay."

"It was a…a family emergency." Emmanuel stares down at his feet.

"When she comes back, please tell her that she left us in good hands," I reply softly.

At first, Emmanuel says nothing. Then, hesitantly, he adds, "She told me you are special people."

"In what way?" I ask.

"She said that from the time you and Mr. Craig got off the plane, you glowed in the love you shared; never once did your eyes leave each other, and you held onto each other as if for dear life."

To be expected. Having been faced with death on too many occasions, we know all too well how dear life can be.

Jack and my eyes meet now. We click our glasses, take a sip, and head back to our hut, drinks in tow.

If we extend our vacation another week, we could break our current lovemaking record.

I'm willing to try. My guess: Jack is, too.

Scaring the parrots isn't the prime objective. We both know this. Instead, it's our creativity in the when, where, and how we do it.

The heat of the mid-day sun has heightened the lagoon's smells. The berry-lush bouquet of heliotrope, in tandem with the heady fragrance of gardenias and the dense scent of plumeria, is the perfect aphrodisiac to stimulate our desire for mutual pleasure.

As Jack's raft floats toward me, I think of all the ways I'll coerce him to please me yet again and what I can do to reciprocate. For example, I could silently swim up to him, awaken him by drizzling his chest with lukewarm droplets, and then allow him to pull me up on the raft beside him. Or very gently, I could ease it beside the dock that juts out beyond our hut and then whisper, "Take me inside…"

I opt for the first scenario. Is the raft strong enough to hold us both?

A much more important question: can it sustain the frenzy of our lust? Or will our thrusts burst it, leaving us grabbing for each other as we gasp for air?

There's only one way to find out.

While one of my hands holds his raft steady, the other moves to Jack's chest, fingers spread wide as it combs through its hairs. When I've reached his taut abdomen, my index finger taunts him as it makes its way downward.

No surprise: Jack is already stiff and ready to play. He tries to pull me up on the raft beside him—

But, instead, he flips it over, and we plummet deep into the lagoon's clear depths.

Like mine, Jack's eyes are open. He grins as he glides my way —

But then something behind me catches his attention, and his smile fades. As he swims over to it, I turn around to see it too:

It's a dead, naked woman.

Tisa.

In the water, her tight dark curls sway with the current. Her eyes are open, but her stare is vacant. No, it is sad.

The chain around her waist is tethered to the scuppered yacht: luxurious and new. I follow Jack, who is swimming around to its stern. We read the vessel's name:

ZERO-SUM GAME
Charlestown, Nevis

By now, my lungs are burning. Jack's must be, too, because he signals me to head to the surface.

We break through the water, gagging for air.

Silently, we mull over what we've discovered.

Realizing what we must do next—alert the resort, then meet with local law enforcement—Jack's groans are loud enough to scare the parrots.

They scatter overhead.

I know what he's thinking:

The honeymoon is over.

2

Yield to Worst

The measurement of the lowest possible yield received on a bond that fully operates within the terms of its contract without defaulting is known as its "yield to worst."

When you think about it, every situation has its yield to worst. For example, you could buy a new outfit but then spill red wine all over it, thus yielding the worst outcome for your wardrobe investment.

There is a bright side: had you drunk the wine instead and then crashed your car into another and totaled it, only to get a ticket or, more embarrassingly, been arrested because the cop on the beat thought you smelled like a drunk, you'd have yielded an even worse outcome.

In other words, "worst" is relative.

"You say you dived into the lagoon, where you saw the body?"

"No." My sigh is loud enough to make Zanzibar's Chief Criminal Investigator, Godfrey Salum, wince.

Instead of just giving our statements, Jack and I were taken into custody in Mkokotoni on Zanzibar's mainland island. After making me cool my heels for thirty minutes, Salum spent an hour interrogating me. Jack is being questioned separately by another investigator, Janeth Othman.

As each minute ticks by, the sky has been darkening steadily as if it's in tune with our moods. I pray Jack is calmer with this line of questioning than I am. Otherwise, we'll spend what's left of our trip here.

For the fifth time—albeit in different ways—CCI Salum has asked me to explain how Jack and I happened to be in the wrong place at the wrong time: underwater near the yacht where Tisa was found tethered. "Five times now, I said my husband and I were lounging on a raft. We were tossed deep into the lagoon when it overturned. Our eyes were open, and we saw Tisa's body tied to the yacht called the Zero-Sum.'"

"And you recognized her immediately?" CCI Salum asks again.

"Yes, of course! Tisa checked us into the resort. She was also our on-call concierge."

"From what our forensics shows, her body had been in the water at least a day," Salum points out. "I cannot imagine you didn't notice that your calls weren't being answered."

"This bit of new knowledge is appreciated, CCI Salum—more so because I'm now bored with the numerous ways you've found to ask the same questions repeatedly."

This time, Salum laughs: deep, from his taut gut.

"I'm glad you find it funny," I mutter. "As it turns out, our cabana was well stocked, so our needs were already well taken care of."

"I'm sure they were."

I'm not too fond of his suggestive tone. "What are you inferring?"

Salum shrugs. "You and your husband may have been the last to see her alive."

"And hearing how unobtrusive she made herself during our stay, exactly how does that make us suspects?" I ask.

Salum smirks. "Many long-time couples come to Kisiwa Cha Paradiso to rekindle a spark of the passion that they once shared. It doesn't always work. On numerous occasions, they turn to those entrusted with making their stay as pleasurable as possible to provide a…let's call it a diversion."

"Are you insinuating that Jack and I invited Tisa to join us in a threesome?"

Worse yet, he's suggesting that I can't satisfy Jack alone?

THE NERVE OF THIS GUY.

I imagine the look on my face is the reason all the blood has left his face.

"My point is that it has happened before." Salum's atonement is shown in hands held up in appeasement. "We hear about it from Parisdiso's concierges all the time."

"Let me assure you, CCI Salum, that my husband and I are fully capable of entertaining ourselves," I growl.

He chuckles. "So I've heard."

"From whom?"

"Emmanuel had, er, mentioned that, from what *he* could hear—I mean, *tell*—you and Mr. Craig kept to yourselves."

"Ah!… Well, it's nice of you to admit my statement has been corroborated," I sniff. "Although I'm disappointed that Emmanuel would tell tales out of school."

"When it comes to his sister, he had every right to divulge what he knows."

"Tisa…*was his sister*? I'm so sorry to hear of his loss." My eyes tear up at the thought. "Considering Jack and I were the ones who informed the staff and the police—and have so graciously consented to be interrogated—I'd say we've not only done our civic duty but have a right to ask a few questions of our own."

"I'm sure your husband is doing just that," Salum declares. "So yes, please, ask away."

"First off, did she drown, or was she already dead when she was tied to the anchor?"

"The fact that there was no water in her lungs indicates she was already dead. There are marks on her neck that indicate she may have died from strangulation."

"Who owned the Zero-Sum Game?" I ask.

"From what we've discovered, it is a corporation based in Switzerland," he concedes.

"Has it been reported missing?"

He glances away. A tell, perhaps? In time, Salum shakes his head. "Not as of yet."

"When will you be towing it out of the lagoon?"

"The yacht is seventy feet long. An adequately equipped tug boat could be in our area within a few days. However, any towing must wait until after the cyclone due to hit within the next forty-eight hours has cleared the area."

"A storm is on its way—now?"

He nods. "Currently, it is a Category Four. Up to 125 mile-an-hour winds are expected."

I grimace at the thought of our paradise lost in dark skies, high tides, and hurricane winds. "A shame since the boat's deterioration would indicate how long it has been scuttled. Did your divers see any signs corroborating my contention that it happened just last night?"

"No, they were not able to determine that." He's yet to look me in the eye.

"Did they search for other bodies?"

A pause, then: "No others were found."

I shift in my seat so that my beach cover-up reveals my bikini top. The sudden movement draws his eyes to me, specifically to my breasts like heat-seeking missiles.

I purr, "Do you like what you see?"

Again, he glances away. "I hope I haven't offended you."

"You wouldn't have—*if you'd answered my questions truthfully*." When he turns to face me, his gawk confirms my accusation.

Salum's phone rings, saving him from answering my

retort. Picking it up, he grunts a "yes, thank you" and hangs up.

"I've still got a few days left of my vacation. I plan to make the most of it. So, frankly, I don't need to hear the reason you're lying about the who, what, and why the boat sank." I stand up. "Enough with these games. You have no reason to hold us."

"Mr. Craig has likewise echoed your opinion to Deputy Investigator Othman." Salum smiles. "And since you've corroborated what he said to her, you're free to go." He stands up and motions for me to do likewise.

Something flickers behind the room's two-way mirror. Now that he knows I'm one of the good guys, I assume whoever was watching feels there is no need to waste more time here.

Though I feel the same way, I must ask: "Why did you hold us for so long?"

"Let's just say that the resort attracts a certain clientele that keeps us on our toes. Your detainment allowed us to initiate a background check. Your Interpol file is impressive—in a good way. I wish I could say the same for others now on the island."

"Do you suspect some bad operatives are on the island now?"

"Yes, unfortunately. And more on the way. We've been informed that several have diplomatic immunity from any occurrences that may shield them from events that may occur while their stay like, say, deaths—be they accidental or like Tisa's, intentional."

"CCI Salum, is this your way of asking me to keep my eyes and ears open on your behalf?"

"You and Mr. Craig will be much more than that. You'll be our first line of defense." His eyes now meet mine head-on. "Ironically, despite your country's help in the creation, training, and ongoing support of Tanzania's elite Critical Response Team, under our country's law, it can only deployed during terrorist threats. However, to mitigate what might become an international incident, your President, Elizabeth Kentfield, has promised ours that you and Mr. Craig can be relied upon for surveillance and protection of the resort staff and other guests, should Kisiwa Cha Paradiso become… I suppose the least egregious metaphor would be untenable."

"But—"

"In any regard, your superiors will soon be in touch with your marching orders. Have a nice day." Salum beams. You'd think he'd just invited me to a garden party.

As if.

So, Libby Kentfield has committed us to police a possible international incident and ruined our vacation?

Yikes. I can only imagine what Jack thinks about *that*.

3

Yacht Insurance

An insurance policy that provides indemnity liability coverage for a sailing vessel is known as yacht insurance. Whereas such insurance will cover gas delivery, towing, and assistance should your yacht get stranded, it also covers the cost of repairing damage to your property and that of others.

By the way, it also protects against bodily injury.

So, yeah, rest assured the bump you put on your hubby's noggin before he fell overboard will eventually be bandaged.

"Jeez! What part of 'on vacation' does Ryan Clancy not understand?" Jack declares.

"Keep your voice down," I implore him.

Not that anyone can hear us. With a cyclone on its way, the street is empty. It takes a a few blocks to find what we're looking for: an old-fashioned British phone booth. From it, we call Acme's toll-free Agents and Assets number. After we give the right password and confirm our fake call names we're put right through.

Even before Ryan speaks, Jack growls, "Don't ask about our tan."

"Frankly, I hadn't planned on it," Ryan admits. "Too much is happening in the real world for me to hear you two whine about your sunburns. And by the way, Emma is patching in DNI Branham, so watch your P's and Q's." He's referring to Emma Honeycutt, our mission team's ComInt director.

"Duly noted," I mutter.

A moment later, we hear a click on the line. Director of National Intelligence Marcus Branham declares, "Sorry to interrupt your vacation, Craigs, but it's for a good cause—or, I should say, to prevent the possibility of a really bad one."

"Explain, sir," Jack says.

"Each year, representatives from various countries' largest financial institutions and their government counterparts convene for a strategy session in an out-of-the-way location," Marcus replies. "This guarantees the privacy they need to discuss issues of importance for safeguarding the world's economic structure. As it so happens, they conveniently chose your vacation spot. Lucky you, eh?"

"No sir," I reply sweetly.

Marcus laughs. "I'd expect your disappointment, Donna. And, truly, I apologize. The folks in question represent two US banks, two from China, two Japanese banks, one from Canada, one from Spain, two British banks, one French bank, and a Swiss bank. Besides glad-handing and listening to guest speakers who will be flown in and out throughout their five-day stay, they'll be massaging their various goals, including sustainable development such as gender, jobs, health, and poverty reduction, which they want to accomplish within this next generation."

"Very admirable," Jack declares with an eye roll. "Still sounds like a sun-and-fun junket to me."

"Your sarcasm aside, Mr. Craig, we've heard chatter from our Russian assets that being perennially excluded from this very important shindig does not sit well with their country's president," Marcus divulges.

"Perhaps he should consider joining that elite country club known as capitalism," Jack retorts.

"Or better yet, give the money he's stolen from his citizens back to them and let them partake in spending it, along with free elections," I add.

"Since that will never happen, it looks like you've got a job for life." Ryan's tone makes it clear: that topic is closed.

"Do we know if Russia is behind it?" Jack asks.

"No. But our asset insists a Russian operative is involved, though in what capacity, we don't yet know," Marcus replies.

"Is the goal a slaughter, or is it to hold the bankers hostage?" I ask.

"Thus far, no goal has been stated, which makes it even more vexing," Marcus admits.

"If everyone who shows up is being vetted, how will the terrorist—or terrorists—infiltrate the forum?" I ask.

"That's an excellent question, and one in which we

have no answer," Marcus concedes. "As you know, the resort is fairly small—no more than thirty cabanas. It's not confirmed yet, but we've been told the banker consortium bought every guest cabana available. Only the thirteen bankers, the two of you, and the keynote speaker will be on the island."

"Do you have the attendee manifest?" Jack asks

"We have. Emma will text your satellite phone the moment we end this call," Ryan assures us.

"First we'll have to pick up a satellite phone. And"—I pause because it's the last thing I want to do—"some munitions."

Jack turns red. "On both counts, I've got us covered."

"*Pardon me?* Are you telling me you brought weapons on what's supposed to be our love fest?" I shake my head in disbelief.

"It was a mistake, believe me," he insists. "I picked up the wrong duffel—the one with the hidden bottom."

"So, what you're telling me is we've got a couple of Sigs and enough slugs to keep a few folks in line, along with two burners, two shortwaves, and a satellite phone?"

"Guilty as charged. But hey, Don: you've got to admit that otherwise, I packed light: sun tan oil, a couple of tank tops and Hawaiian shirts, shorts, a couple of drawstring pants. Not even a razor!" Jack runs my hand over his scruff.

I have to grin. "And that Speedo hasn't seen the light of day since we've been here."

He snorts. "You know I'm a swim trunks guy."

"You haven't worn those either," I remind him.

"Only because you insist I go *au natural*. Then again

what's good for the goose is good for the gander." Jack's boyish grin never fails to melt my heart.

"Too much information, folks!" Ryan growls.

"Well, given the mission we're now tasked with, here's a bit of intel you may want to know: having a satellite phone means we'll be breaking the island's ironclad rule against bringing any forms of communication with us," I warn them. "It may get us banned from paradise."

"Doubtful, since I suspect everyone else will too," Marcus counters. "As that old saying goes, 'There's no rest for the weary international banker. Just don't get caught, okay?"

"Cross our hearts," I vow.

"Marcus, I don't know if Ryan told you, but our resort concierge was just killed. If we're assigned a new one, the person will definitely be a suspect," Jack points out. "For that matter, it won't be great if he or she makes us before we make them."

"If Emmanuel doesn't go into mourning, why don't we request him?" I suggest. "The victim was his sister. He'll be determined to see justice done. If need be, we recruit him to our cause."

"Not a bad idea, Ryan admits. "But only if the right circumstance presents itself."

"Got it, chief," I assure him. "By the way, though the yacht was registered in the Caribbean island of Nevis, its ownership is tied to LLC based in Switzerland. However, the local authorities couldn't break the corporate veil on the yacht's ownership."

"There is only one banker from Switzerland: Oskar Surbeck," Ryan points out. "I'll have Emma search yacht sales records. Maybe she can pull up photos of the boat or Surbeck in regattas, yachting news, or social media. If not, we'll put Arnie on it," Ryan replies.

Arnie Locklear, our mission team's tech operative, is a white-hat hacker with black-hat skills.

We hear Emma declare, "On it, boss!"

Ryan sighs. "Speaking of your mission team, Arnie has a question for you."

Jack looks at his watch. "He better make it quick. If we don't catch the last ferry to the island, we'll have to swim there."

Emma, married to Arnie, shouts, "Yo, dude—it's now or never!"

By the way Arnie is panting, it's obvious our tech operative is running over. "Hey, while you're on the island, can you bring Nicky a coconut head?"

Jack groans. "You mean, one of those ugly ones with a face carved on it?"

"Exactly! But not too scary. More cute. Maybe an animal—"

"Yeah, okay, gotta go." Jack slams down the phone. "Well, that was productive."

The ferry's warning bellows have us running to the dock.

And st il l, we miss t he fer ry.

"Damn it!" Jack doubles over to catch his breath. "I told you not to wear those sandals."

"No—in fact, your exact words were "those heels

make your legs sexy.' Of course, that was before I broke one trying to keep up with you." I take off the shoe in question.

"He's right." The voice with the deep midland Texas accent comes from a yacht on a nearby berth.

I glance over to its owner: a very buff, very tanned guy. His gaze drops to my legs but slowly makes its way up until our eyes meet.

His grin shows he likes what he sees.

I smile back. And why not? He's got a boat—a really nice one. I'd have no problem at all cruising over in a sun-kissed orange 65-foot Sunseeker Sports Yacht. Maybe he'll put it to good use in our honor.

I start by playing dumb. "Aw, gee! Was that the last ferry?" I punctuate my concern with a pout.

"Sorry, but yes." He hikes a leg on the boat's aft side —the better to rest an elbow on a knee and get an even closer look at me. "Where are you headed?"

"Not far. Just over there." I point to Kisiwa Cha Paradiso.

Buff and Tan chuckles. "Ya don't say! Why, I'm headed there myself."

I coo, "Ya don't say! It's a small world, after all."

"And getting smaller all the time," he replies. "The name's Rufus Coulter. Hop onboard."

"Don't mind if we do." Jack's tone could be a tad less gruff. Still, he holds out his hand and receives a hardy handshake.

We've just clamored over the side when we hear, "Yoohoo, Rufus! We're here! Sorry we are late, mon ami!" The voice, female, has a breathy French accent.

The woman calling him is slim but buxom with a luxurious head of auburn tresses. The "we" she refers to includes two other women. Like her, they are slim leggy tall twenty-somethings—

And gorgeous.

"Ah, here's the rest of my party!" Rufus winks knowingly at me. "In reality, they're divorcées."

"Ya don't say." Suddenly, I feel creased. And saggy And threatened. "I thought your name sounded familiar. You're Rufus Coulter, the divorce attorney to the rich and famous."

"Guilty as charged." He hurries over to help his clients on board, then signals the boat's captain to start the engine.

As the yacht backs away from the dock, Rufus adds, "Did you know that this island resort is renowned for having the speediest relationship-settlement laws in the world? A mere seventy-two hours!"

"Ya don't say," I murmur.

"Yep, I do. So, you'll see us around while my lovely clients' settlements are processed and finalized." Rufus scans the darkening sky. "Weather permitting, the judge flies in on the last day to grant the final decree." He nods toward the other women. "Do you recognize them?"

I look beyond him to Jack, who sits on the yacht's bow. He's got the well-endowed diamond-dripping redhead on one side of him and the tall, wraithlike almond-eyed brunette beauty on the other.

Is it just me, or are these ladies hungrily eyeing Jack as if he were the last hors d'oeuvre on a cater waiter's platter?

Except for the third woman: blonde. She's so disinterested that she's moved to the boat's cabin and has closed the door behind her.

I ask Rufus: "The woman with the auburn hair is in one of the *'Hot Housewives'* TV reality shows. Am I right?"

"Yes ma'am. That's Sabine Dubois, from one of the international franchises."

"Let me guess: Paris."

Rufus nods. "*Oui,* madame, and all that implies. The producers couldn't have picked a more idyllic city: ooh-lah-lah views of the Seine and its many bridges and *maisonettes* upholstered to the hilt in Louis-the-Fourteenth's castoffs by haute couture-clad cast of couples and their requisite lovers: misters and mistresses who provide additional eye candy."

Gag me.

I realize Rufus is scrutinizing me bow to stern. And yes, he's also undressing me with his eyes. To get his attention, I snap my fingers in his face. "My face is up here, dude."

Still curious, he asks, "Speaking of which: weren't you a 'Hot Housewife' yourself?"

I chuckle. "Guilty as charged."

"Don't tell me…" He taps the side of his noggin to prove the memory is in there somewhere. "I got it! You were with the *'Hot Housewives of Hilldale!'*"

"Wow! I'm surprised you know it."

"Of course I remember it—and you. All of the *Hot Housewives* franchises are my client hunting grounds. Talk about shooting ducks in a barrel! And Hubby the

Hunk over there. In fact, of all the ho's, you were my favorite!"

"I beg your pardon?" If my gritted teeth aren't enough of a tip-off, the fact that I'm flicking my nails—which are sharp enough to perforate his jugular—should warn him there will be a penance for a crack like that.

He smells danger. Holding up his hands, he adds, "Not 'ho,' as in 'whore,' but *H-H-O-H*, as in the TV reality series, *'Hot Housewives of Hilldale.'* It's what true fans called it despite the show's claim to fame as being the most short-lived reality series in history."

"Not to mention one with almost the highest body count," I point out.

"Ah! So, the write-up in *People* was true—you know, about real bombs in the boobs?" He winks at me. "Inquiring minds want to know."

"Let me put it this way—all's well that ends well."

"Dang it, lady! You're ruining my trip down *HHOH* Memory Lane." Rufus shrugs. "Granted, I understand why someone might want to kill that Penelope Bing person. Talk about a bitchy banshee! But considering the ratings were through the roof—even after that last episode's blackout—why did the network kill the series?"

"Wasn't the premise of on-air death and destruction reason enough?"

"Hey, when it comes to TV, that's what sells, isn't it?"

"You're right there." I nod toward the brunette, who's now taken the best seat in the house: my husband's lap. "I've seen her before too but I can't place her."

"She's a supermodel. Her name is Xiãng Fong McDinty, but by the end of the week, she'll have lost the

Scottish half of that double barrel. The sphincter on a tight end with the Detroit Lions is going to seal tighter than a gnat's ass when he realizes how much her settlement is costing him." Rufus shrugs. "Maybe he'll luck out, and she'll be too stoned to sign it."

I glance over at her. "She does look a bit glassy-eyed. But isn't that just her blue-steel runway stare?"

He snorts. "I wish! Xiãng likes zoning out so much that she took a pharmacology course on zombie drugs. She mixes downers as if they're designer cocktails…Hey, don't laugh! Hand to God, I'm being serious. She puts them in vials and lines them up on a shelf, like party favors, then says, 'Down the hatch, folks! All in good fun!' He shakes his head in wonder. "And yet, she can still saunter down a runway with her eyes closed. Go figure."

"The sign of a true artist," I murmur.

"I'll say!" Just then, our captain guns the engine. Rufus nearly loses his footing.

As our yacht ducks and dodges other boats on its way out to the open sea, I ask, "Who's the blond woman who went below deck?"

"Yulia Tarasova. Descended from a long line of White Russians—and I don't mean the drink. Speaking of which, I wouldn't mind one right about now." Just the thought has him licking his lips.

"Interesting." *Not.* Especially since Jack will have to vet her. "She's Russian?"

"Yes, ma'am. But she's now resettled in the South of France. It's where she met her current husband. Wealthy as Croesus." Gleefully, he rubs his hands. "The settlement is equal to my last ten years of fees, easy."

During the rest of the short boat ride, Rufus probes me on which of the *HHOH*s I've kept in contact with.

"None," I emphasize.

"And to think I thought y'all would end up as thick as thieves, what with such a bonding experience of putting your relationships under a nationally televised microscope." He sighs longingly. "I'd have loved to have handled the divorces that came out of that shit show!"

You'd have been better off serving as *HHOH*'s official undertaker," I reply, "Seeing how Patty's husband, James, died from a self-inflicted gunshot wound and Ariel was married to a terrorist who blew himself up."

He whistles. "What about the others?"

"It turns out that Roger's fiancée, Sienna, was a Russian spy. "

"Go figure! But given Penelope Bing's antics, her marriage to Peter couldn't have lasted after *HHOH*," Rufus counters.

"That ship has sailed," I inform him. "He left her, not the other way around."

"Dang it! I knew I should have kept in touch with him! With the Q Score Penelope had by the end of the show, my fee on her settlement would have been through the roof!"

Should I break the news that she's wasted her fame and fortune on bad choices—including her investment in the Hilldale sex boutique, Cum & Get It? Nah. When the mighty fall, leave them some shred of decency: in Penelope's case, crotchless panties and a couple of pasties.

Thankfully, Rufus takes note that we're now a few yards from Kisiwa Cha Paradiso's dock and he's got clients to wrangle. I'm surprised to see Emmanuel waiting to greet Rufus's arrival with several other concierges and golf carts to whisk the guests to their cabanas. As one would imagine, Emmanuel looks forlorn. Still, he forces his lips into a meek smile.

Rufus helps his clients onto the gangplank: first, Sabine, then Xiǎng, who pulls Jack along.

He glances back and mouths, *Sorry.*

Rufus chuckles. "I wouldn't keep the home fires burning if you catch my drift."

"I do. And believe me, I'm not worried."

"A shame. I was looking forward to adding you to my client roster. You're still revered as a take-no-prisoners warrior wife in the Hot Housewives fan clubs."

Playfully, I pinch his cheek. "If I didn't know better, I'd say you're the jealous one."

His laughter comes out in a roar. "*Me?* Hardly! That little lady is insatiable. I'm just the most convenient notch on her very long belt"—he nods toward Jack—"which he'll soon smart from."

"Not to worry. Jack doesn't take such liaisons seriously."

"What?… Ah! You thought I meant that as a figure of speech, eh? I was referring to Xiǎng's handiwork." The next thing I know, he's lifted his shirt. His back is crisscrossed with still swollen whelps. "Those nails of hers are just as lethal as yours. One of my clients who was also booked for this trip refused to come because Xiǎng threatened to scratch her eyes out."

"And you still want her as a client?"

"To make the big bucks, I suck it up." Casually, Rufus leans against the boat—

But then jumps back with a yelp. "Okay, full disclosure: clients expect some handholding—or even more." He rolls his eyes. "It's not like I didn't know what I was getting into. Tight End's lawyers took pictures of the scars she put on his back." He shrugs. "But he knew what he was getting into when he married her, right? And you'd be surprised how many men are into that sort of thing—especially at the hands of the famous."

"Not really," I murmur.

Ouch. Jack will find out the hard way: this is not a vacation.

Before coming on deck, Yulia waits until the other divorcées are about to head off on their concierge-driven golf carts. As she walks off with Rufus, her eyes fall on Xiăng and Jack. But then she must feel my stare because she turns to look straight at me. When our eyes meet, she shrugs, raises her hood over her head, and strides over to the cart that will whisk her and her luggage away.

Jack will have his hands full with too many others—

And for all the wrong reasons.

4

After-Hours Trading

After-hours trading is securities trading that starts at 4 p.m. U.S. (Eastern Time) because that is after the major U.S. stock exchanges close. These trading sessions can run as late as 8 p.m., though volume typically thins out much earlier in the session.

Trading in the after-hours is conducted through ECNs (which stands for "electronic communication networks.")

You don't have to be in the financial sector to partake in after-hours trading. Ask any call girl, and she'll tell you how much money can be made on Wall Street after hours—

In the closest and fanciest bars and hotel lounges.

I wait until Rufus and Yulia ride away with their concierges before greeting Emmanuel. "Can we talk in private?"

"Of course, madame." He points to the path that takes us to his office. "Follow me."

Neither speaks. When we arrive, he murmurs to his assistant that we are not to be disturbed and ushers me into a large office, shutting the door behind us.

"No need to worry, Emmanuel. We are pleased with our cabana and our stay," I assure him. "I just wanted to express my condolences for the loss of your sister."

My words stun him. When I sit and motion for him to do the same, he does so reluctantly. He puts a hand in his jacket pocket but says nothing.

My heart breaks for Emmanuel—all the more reason I must convince him that not only will we help him bring Tisa's killer to justice, but we'll save his life too, and those of all who are here on the island.

It's up to me to break the ice. "I cannot even imagine the pain you must be going through. Do you have any idea who might have done this to her?"

Warily, he shakes his head.

"Having found her body, we were interrogated by the Tanzanian police." I lean in. "Emmanuel, because Tisa was your sister, I imagine you'd like to bring her killer to justice."

His eyes narrow. "I do. Why do you ask?"

"Jack and I want to help."

"I… I appreciate your offer. But…I don't see how you can."

"Our professions are—well, I guess you'd call it monitoring criminal activity that may have international repercussions. When law enforcement authorities in Zanzibar learned of this, we were asked to be on alert at Kisiwa Cha Paradiso. It has intel that a terrorist attack is imminent. The targets are the international bankers who have convened here."

Though taken aback, Emmanuel nods slowly. "Then you know who else is on the island?"

"Yes. And, as you saw, we were graciously given a ride to the island by those guests who've come to complete their divorce settlements."

"How would you help, Mrs. Craig?"

"We will vet your visitors and staff for discrepancies that earmark them as terrorists."

He shifts uncomfortably in his chair. "And if you find these discrepancies, how will you proceed? I ask because the resort has a reputation to uphold. It's why we do a deep vetting of our staff. Obviously, we can't do the same for our guests."

"If we're successful, we'll remove the perpetrators from the island as discreetly as possible," I explain.

A long minute goes by. Finally, Emmanuel sighs. "No need to worry about our employees. I assure you nothing is more important than the security of our guests. It starts with the staff entrusted to serve them. I know firsthand the rigors of our corporation's background checks. It is extensive, as is fitting for a world-class resort."

"It will be easier if our cover is as part of the resort's staff."

Emmanuel frowns. "Madame, what you request would give my employer grounds for my dismissal."

"If your sister's death doesn't encourage you to work with us, what will?"

"Of course it does." Emmanuel stares out the window at the darkening sky. Sighing, he says, "Fair warning: our guests expect every pleasure as a service." His emphasis validates what Jack and I may have to do.

"By that, you mean that some guests require services that are intimate in nature."

Emmanuel nods. "Yes. After all, we are a full-service resort."

"In those cases, allow us to accommodate that service too," I reply.

His hesitant nod shows he gets my meaning. "Well then, those services are indicated by two asterisks after the words 'massage' or 'towels.'"

"Less than subtle, but to be expected," I reply.

"All I ask in return is that you keep me informed when you're in another guest's room, with or without their permission," he warns. "That way, I can cover for you should you be discovered searching their belongings. Otherwise, the resort's reputation will be in tatters. All the more reason your process of elimination must be *discreet*."

"Understandable."

Resigned by our new reality, he sighs. "I'll inform our CEO of the situation and your offer for protection."

I smile. "Ah! So, there is a satellite phone on the island!"

Emmanuel shrugs. "And my computer also has satellite capability for administrative and operations functions. Also, in case of an emergency." He grimaces. "Now we have two. Besides what you suspect, the latest weather report upgraded the incoming storm to a Category 5 cyclone. It is moving quickly our way. We can anticipate hundred-and-eighty mile-an-hour winds. I've already warned my corporate office that communication will be spotty at best."

"Can you get me a list of the guests and a map of the lagoons where their cabanas are located?"

Emmanuel taps on his electronic pad. A moment later, I hear a ping on my mobile phone.

"As requested, you now have access to all our guests' dossiers," he explains. "As you pointed out, except for your party of two and those here for their divorces, the other guests are here for the international banking symposium. Tap on the map of all the island's cabanas. They are labeled with the guests' names. The photos taken upon the guests' arrival are also included."

The photo taken of Jack and me comes to mind. To think that was just a week ago! With what has happened today, it seems like a year has passed.

To keep things upbeat, I say, "I found that to be a considerate gesture on the resort's behalf."

Emmanuel smiles. "Yes, it is a sweet remembrance. But, in truth, its real purpose is to assist the concierges in memorizing our guests' faces so that we always get their names correct as well as document your, well, 'predilections.'"

"I see." Well, there goes the magic.

"When summoned, you're to drop off this complimentary gift box, which the event's directors created especially for their guests." He hands it to me. "Less personal than the resort's usual offering, and certainly more in line with a business symposium of bankers."

I open it. "I'll say," I murmur. Inside are several

expensive and functional items: a Cartier pen, a miniature electronic notepad, and a Patek Philippe watch.

Emmanuel moves beside me. A map of the island is now on his electronic pad. "Here is your lagoon, nicknamed Happy Parrot. The international bankers are assigned cabanas around the island's largest lagoon, designated Turquoise. It is to the northwest side of yours. There is a shortcut on this path, here"—he points to it—"between these two hillsides. And here is where their meetings are to be held. The times listed beside the guest's name are special requests they've already made, including the optimum delivery time."

I peruse the guest manifest:

Event Coordinators:
- Gretta Ullman (F: Zurich, Switzerland) Turquoise Lagoon, #1 (6:30 pm Fresh Fruit)
- Phillip Warburton (M: Fort Worth TX, USA) Turquoise Lagoon, #2

Chinese Bankers:
- Chen Mùchén (M: Beijing) Turquoise Lagoon, #A (5 pm: Five Chocolate Milkshakes; make on-premises, and leave in freezer.**)
- Hu Gang (M: Beijing) Turquoise Lagoon, #B (midnight Massage **)

US Bankers:
- Krebs, Howard (New York, NY US) Turquoise Lagoon, #E (11 pm Catering Cart)

• Morton, Edgar Randall, III (Philadelphia, PA, US)
Turquoise Lagoon, #F (See Krebs)

Japanese Bankers:
• Shimizu, Hikaru (Tokyo, JP; M) Turquoise Lagoon, #G
(8pm extra towels)
• Gima, Arisa (Kyoto, JP; F) Turquoise Lagoon, #H

German Bankers:
• Hans (Berlin, Germany) Turquoise Lagoon,#I
(**10**pm; Deliver Schorschbräu Schorschbock 57)
• Gűnther (Munich, Germany) Turquoise Lagoon,#J

British Bankers:
• Smythe-Brantley, Reginald (Sir; London, UK)
Turquoise Lagoon, #K (7:30 pm Deliver sealed folio)
• Hodgson-Payne, Colin (Sir; London, UK) Turquoise
Lagoon, #L (See Above)

French Banker:
• Micheaux (M: Paris, FR); Turquoise Lagoon
(6 pm Deliver Champagne**)

Canadian Banker:
• Blaine Wentworth (Vancouver, BC, CN)
Turquoise Lagoon, #O (8:30 pm Extra pillows)

Swiss Banker:
Surbeck, Oskar (Zurich, Switzerland) Turquoise Lagoon,
#P (5:30 pm: Extra towels **)

Spanish Banker:
Claudio Cervantes (Madrid, Spain) Turquoise Lagoon, (7 pm Fresh Shrimp)

Guest X: High Chief's Cabana, Royal Lagoon (arriving within 24 hours.)

The resort put the Chinese bankers at one end and the Americans at another. A diplomatic move? My guess is yes.

"How many of the conference's attendees are already here?" I ask.

Emmanuel glances down at his watch. "All except one. The keynote speaker will have arrived by midnight."

Scanning the map, I look for the cabana designated for the conference's keynote speaker, denoted merely as "Guest X."

"Why is this guest's name left blank?" I ask.

Emmanuel glances at the folder in my hand. "The name is being withheld at the event planners' behest."

We'll see about that.

I nod and say nothing. Nonchalantly, I ask, "Did this person make it to the island before the storm?"

"No. But I've been told to expect this guest within the next twelve hours: several hours before the storm is predicted to land. As soon as I'm given the name, you will know also. That way, you may do your, er, reconnaissance."

"Has this sort of privacy been requested previously?"

"No. A VIP booking may be given under an assumed name, but in time, the VIP's handler divulges enough of their boss's preferences that we can figure it out. Unfortunately, not this time." Emmanuel sighs. "It doesn't bother me. Considering what I've seen of guests here at the resort, I've come to expect anything."

That gives me something to chuckle over.

But the smile is wiped off my face when I scan further down the list. Lucky Jack! The four cabanas assigned to Rufus and his trio of beauties are in the next cove over from ours. He won't have to go too far for his undercover ops.

I ask, "What about the divorcées and their lawyer, Mr. Coulter?"

"He's resigned to be at their beck and call." Emmanuel blushes. "However, Monsieur Coulter made it quite explicit that he would only do so until midnight. Should they have requests between then and eight in the morning, I should send a male concierge who I deem, in his words, 'up to the task.' Mr Craig would ably fit the bill."

"Got it." In other words, Jack will be called into duty. This trip gets better and better. "Do those in Mr. Coulter's party also get courtesy gift boxes?"

"Yes, albeit the items are a bit more…well, Let's just say they are personalized, per Mr. Coulter's request." He opens one so that I can see what he means. Each box holds barely-there lingerie, a scented lubricant, a dildo, handcuffs, and the miniature digital pad in pink. The last three items are inscribed with the recipient's name.

"Classy," I murmur.

Emmanuel chuckles.

"You'll have to verify Jack and me to the coordinators, Gretta and Phillip, as the concierge assigned to bring welcome gifts to the banking event's guests," I say.

"I'll send them a note now," Emmanuel assures me. He goes to a closet and pulls out a tote bag, which he fills with several caftans like the ones used by the female concierge staff. They are turquoise with a white floral design. "These are for you. For Monsieur Craig, I've also included a few tee shirts and our signature sweatpants." The men's tees are white, but the pants are turquoise. He puts a few of each in the tote as well.

I rise and hold out my hand. "I won't take any more of your time."

I'll walk you to your cabana. You'll need help dragging those carts."

He's not kidding. There are two of them. One holds towels, miniature battery-operated lamps, massage oils, bath salts, and several of the female concierges' colorful caftans. Another, with a refrigerated compartment, has food and various drinks: fruit juices, wines, sodas, and water bottles.

And then there are the guests' gift boxes.

After we take the cart to my cabana, Emmanuel adds, "I have an extra box if you'd like one for yourself." He walks to a cabinet, pulls two out, and hands it to me.

"Thanks! I'm sure it will come in handy."

Emmanuel nods. "Yes, that is my hope."

He bids me good luck. His furrowed brow is proof he's worried for my safety. We shake hands. His grip is firm enough to make me wince. Is it a sign of desperation or appreciation?

I pray the latter.

"Thanks." I try to sound like I mean it. Who knows? It may be the best souvenir I get from this trip.

If anything, the negligee may come in handy.

But first things first: we'll have to get off this island.

Realizing I should upload copies to Acme. I head to the closet, where Jack stored his duffel—

But it's gone.

What the hell?

Was Jack invited to join the divorcée entourage permanently?

If so, at the very least, he should have left me half of our go-bag stash.

When he resurfaces, he'd better have a good excuse.

5

Zombies

A *"zombie" company is what you'd expect: one barely earning enough money to continue operating but unable to pay off its debts.*

Overhead (wages, rent, and interest payments on the company) and debt are high. Perhaps access capital is not available, and poor revenue performance keeps financial angels from bailing it out or from banks seeing it as viable for a loan.

Barely ahead of insolvency, it's on life support.

Eventually, it'll be put out of its misery.

Folks, we've all lived through this scenario before.

Stockholders: be very scared! Run for your lives!

To distract myself from thinking about what Jack is doing and with whom, I study the guests' dossiers for likely targets, of which there are many. Their likes and dislikes in food, people, and activities are also described.

Besides a request delivery, I'll need to figure out how to distract them so that I can search their cabanas for anything that can turn the island into a bloodbath or a nuclear waste dump.

Oh, fun.

First up on my agenda is Chen Múchèn of Beijing's International Capital. Múchèn loves eating and has the belly to prove it. He partakes in covert sugar fixes. But because he doesn't want his competitors to view his sweet tooth as a weakness, he's ordered chocolate milkshakes to be delivered to his cabana before dinner. His next scheduled shake is at five o'clock this afternoon, which gives me an hour to prepare how to deliver it and search his room.

It would be easier if Jack or I provided a distraction while the other searched for clues.

Just where the hell is Jack?

As if reading my mind, he bounds up the steps of our cabana.

"Well, well, look who's back," I huff.

He puts up his hands as if surrendering to my angst. "But, unfortunately, not for long."

"And why is that?"

"I promised Xiāng I'd give her a massage."

"I'll bet you did," I retort. "By the way, what did you do with the go-bag?"

Jack stares at me. Then he heads over to the closet. Seeing its absence for himself, he turns to me, angered. He motions me to look for telltale signs of surveillance: listening or video devices secreted in knickknacks, light fixtures, or vents.

A fifteen-minute search uncovers six eyes and ears. We block their signals by tilting the eyes toward dead spaces and putting the ears next to white noise—easy enough to do, given the rush of wind created by the pending storm.

When we're done, I mutter, "The fact that the bag was stolen is evidence our comings and goings are being watched. Well, at least it justified your time with Xiāng." I sigh. "I assume you have a similar game plan for all the ladies?"

"Whether you—or I—like it or not, yes—just like you'll have to distract the men while I search their rooms." Jack leans his head against mine. "Look, like you, I thought we'd gotten away from all of this for two weeks. But with the storm on its way, those on this island who are innocent will be sitting ducks. For that matter, so will we, unless we do something about it."

"I filled Emmanuel in on the situation," I assure him.

Jack raises his head to stare me in the eye. "That was risky, considering he has keys to all the cabanas and knows the island like the back of his hand."

"He lost a sister. I took a guess he'd want to avenge her death. Turns out I was right." I take the guest manifests off the coffee table and hand it to Jack. "It's going to be an arduous process of elimination. If we're to find the terrorists before the event begins—let alone before the storm arrives—we'll need to be quick. Here's tonight's agenda."

Jack scans it. Gawking, he exclaims, "We're to vet everyone—all seventeen banking guests—*tonight*? And before the storm hits?"

"Seems like it, so we better get busy. These dossiers list everyone's cabana location as well as a concierge request. While one of us delivers it and distracts the target, the other can search and seize."

"There's one upside to our reconnaissance: they don't know we're onto them," I argue. "We have an advantage as long as they think they're incognito. So let's use it."

Jack shrugs. "If you say so. Okay, who's our first target?"

"One of the Chinese bankers—a guy named Chen Múchèn." I show Jack Múchèn's dossier.

Reading it, Jack gawks. "He's into chocolate milk-shakes—*while having sex?*"

"Don't remind me." I shudder. "And quit staring at me with pity."

Jack's eyes roam to the clock on the wall. "That still leaves an hour for me to distract Xiāng."

Ugh.

Suddenly, I remember what Rufus told me: "Hey, did you know Xiāng is into zombie drugs? According to Rufus, she downs them like Red Bull. She claims it gives her 'staying power.' While you're keeping her busy, I can steal enough of it for our targets." Just saying that makes me want to gag in my mouth.

"It would make it easier to search their rooms," Jack points out. He stands up. "Well, let's get this over with."

I stroke his cheek. "Hey, if you're lucky, she may be knocked out when you get there, and all you'll have to do is leave a note that says, 'Thanks for the memories.'"

"Ha, ha, very funny."

Not really. Still, it's reassuring to know he feels that way about it.

Before we leave, we litter the cabana with travel tradecraft—cereal under the welcome mat that can be crushed, a paper clip that will drop from the top of a door if it's opened—so that we're clued into any more home invasions.

That way, if our saboteur returns, we'll know as soon as we enter.

Jack takes off first. I wait twenty minutes and then follow.

The divorcées are assigned to Flamingo Lagoon. Xiãng's cabana is on its far side. Unlike the other cabanas, which are dark, her windows flicker with candlelight.

As I suspected, the door is unlocked. Maybe Jack left it that way. Or maybe it's Xiãng's way to remind the others that they are always welcome to her never-ending party or because she forgot to turn the bolt in her perpetually drug-induced state. In any regard, I'm able to slip right in.

Hard rock blares from the cabana's sound system, an old-school bad-boy anthem that, in its day, was favored by head-bobbing stoners channeling the lead guitarist's ecstatic joy while thrusting lustily against his guitar.

It also provides the tempo for Xãing's grunts and clinches as, with eyes wide shut, she straddles her latest conquest.

I'm too heartbroken to verify that it's Jack.

Instead, I scan the room for her vial stash. As Rufus predicted, it's on the table next to the kitchen. The vials are arranged in each place setting like party favors.

If she inadvertently opens her eyes, I get down on my hands and knees and crawl slowly toward the table. I'm just a few feet away when someone grabs my foot and yanks it so hard that I land on my belly.

The next thing I know, I'm pinned to the floor. When I lift my head, a hand is slapped over my mouth.

In my ear, my captor hisses, "Surprise, surprise."

It's Jack.

At first, I'm relieved. But then, I ask myself:

Who is Xiãng riding like a bronco-buster?

As if reading my mind, Jack whispers, "Poor Rufus!"

My stillness convinces Jack to let me slip out from under him.

Rising into a crouch, Jack nods for me to follow him. When we reach the table, he grabs two fistfuls of vials and hands them to me. I put them in my tote as he sweeps up even more small bottles, putting them in his jacket pocket.

Jack heads for the closet and the bathroom while I go through her dresser and then back into the living room, scrounging for any place that might conceal weapons.

I find nothing except even more vials, her stash of pills, and a mortar and pestle.

In time, Jack signals me it's time for us to skedaddle.

Silent like mice, we crawl out of the cabana.

6

Overnight Swap Index

When an overnight rate is exchanged for a fixed interest rate, this financial dealing is called an "overnight index swap."

The "floating leg" of this transaction is the federal funds rate.

The "fixed leg" is the agreed-upon rate between the parties involved, which is accounted for in the swap's value to each party.

The interest of the overnight rate portion is compounded and paid by both parties on the rest of the dates.

You'd think the words "leg" and "party" in a sentence would be intriguing, right? I've just proven that this is not always the case.

When we're safely back at our cabana, we twist open the tops on each of the juices, sodas, and water and put in several drops of Xiãng's zombie cocktail. Afterward, we inject the sedative through the corks of the wine and champagne bottles.

When we're done, I pull the electronic notepad with the dossiers from its hiding place—zipped into the middle of a couch pillow's stuffing. I turn it on and hand it to Jack.

I show him the list of concierge requests and the guests' photos, starting with the first one on our list: Chen Mùchén.

As we put on our concierge uniforms, Jack snickers at Chen Mùchén's request. "Seriously? This dude wants five chocolate milkshakes—for himself?"

"As long as it gives you enough time to search, ours is not to reason why," I point out. I've specifically omitted the "do or die" part of that saying. Why invite bad luck?

I head to the kitchen, where I've stored the ingredients given for Mùchén's shakes: ice cream, chocolate syrup, whipped cream, and then the most essential ingredient of all: a vial of the zombie cocktail. I hold it up to the light. "How much of this should I use?"

Jack frowns. "Your guess is as good as mine. Xiãng shakes a few drops onto her tongue. It gives her a buzz. But she's built up a tolerance and is a little slip of a thing."

"Whereas Mùchén is built like the Mighty Hulk," I point out. "I may have to use half a vial."

"Just don't kill him—especially if he's innocent."

"Sure, okay, whatever." Jack points at the manifest. "By the way, what do the asterisks mean?"

"Oh yeah, those…" I sigh. "The guest expects…you know… *sex*."

He gazes down at Mùchén's photo. "Ah!… Well….Good luck with that."

"What?…" I stare down at the line indicated by his finger. "That…wasn't there before!"

"It is now." Jack's eyes hold pity. "Do you think he'll want his, er, 'massage' before or after the shakes?"

"Just work fast. Trust me, I'll figure out some excuse to get out of there," I mutter.

"Will do," Jack promises.

I've barely knocked on the cabana when the door flings open.

The stereo blares the retro tune, *Shimmy Shimmy KoKo Bop* by Little Anthony and the Imperials:

Sittin' in a native hut
Wonderin' what to do
Along came a native girl
Did a native dance
It was like in paradise
Put me in a trance
Goin' shimmy, shimmy ko-ko-bop…

"You've surely taken your sweet time." Mùchén's English is tinged with a British inflection and the arrogance of someone used to bullying underlings. By how his eyes sweep over me, he's added me to what I imagine is a very long list of those he's put in that category.

I hand over his storm lamps and his gift box. The former is dismissed out of hand, but the latter gets an approving nod. When he opens it and sees what's inside, he smiles, puts on the watch, and then holds it out to admire it.

Lowering my eyes, I murmur, "Forgive me, sir. If you allow me, I'll whip up your milkshakes post haste."

"The sooner the better." Mùchén's sneer is delivered with an all-over gaze. While steering me toward the cabana's kitchen, he places his hand on the small of my back. But it doesn't stay there for long. A not-so-gentle pat on my backside is a not-so-subtle reminder of my true purpose there: to provide a different kind of sugar fix.

Not if I can help it.

One by one, to the rhythm of the music, I take ingredients out of the cart, lining them up on the counter: a gallon of chocolate ice cream, heavy cream, a squirt jar filled with fudge sauce, whipped cream, Maraschino cherries, straws, and a blender. With the skill of a mixologist and the moves of a *Hullaballoo* dancer, I add the first three ingredients to the blender, bopping my head to the beat of the song. Then I do the unexpected: I grab a banana from Mùchén's fruit bowl and peel it like a strip tease. When the peel is off, I break pieces of banana and drop them into the blender until one bite-size morsel remains.

I hold it out to Mùchén. His mouth opens, ready to accept it, But I shake my head.

"On your knees," I coo.

He obeys. Does he do so out of hunger or subservience? Does it matter?

Of course not—as long as Jack has enough time to search the premises.

Sleight of hand—my right—pours half the contents of the zombie vial into the blender while my left-hand tosses the banana tidbit at him.

Am I surprised Mùchén catches it in his mouth? Not at all.

Moving back behind the counter, I start the blender. Its sound must bring Mùchén to orgasm because he trembles and groans.

I place six tall glasses on the counter in a row. Then I drizzle fudge into the bottom of each. I also swirl it on their sides. Taking the blended ingredients, I pour equal amounts into each glass, add a dollop of whipped cream, and finally top each with a cherry.

Greedily, Mùchén gulps one down. "Your turn," he says.

I fake a lady-like sip of another shake.

I guess this isn't what he has in mind because before I know it, my caftan is ripped from my body. He takes one of the other milkshakes and pours it over my breasts.

"Now, that's more like it!" he declares.

Like hell it is.

When he bends down to lick them, my slap stuns him—

But not for long. He slaps back—

And I reel against the counter, toppling the rest of the milkshakes.

Which is precisely where he wants me. He forces me face down and kicks my legs open—

Only to flop on top of me.

He snores in my ear.

I do my best to wriggle out from under him, but I'm pinned beneath his bulk.

Worse yet, I'm suffocating. Weakly, I gasp, "Help…"

Now the snores are accompanied by grunts—Jack's, as he shoves Mùchén onto the floor.

I fall, too. At least I land on top of my attacker.

Gasping, I roll off. "Did you find anything incriminating?"

Not a thing—unless you consider a suitcase filled with Snickers bars and food porn mags—*Bon Appetite, Food & Wine, Taste of Home, Rich Table, Bake from Scratch*—a reason to arrest him."

"Then let's go back to our cabana so I can change," I say. "He won't screech about the mess unless he's willing to admit to attempted rape."

"You had me at 'go,'" Jack replies.

"What time is it?" I ask.

"A quarter to six."

"I have to deliver a bottle of champagne to Alain Micheaux by six o'clock," I explain. "He's the French banker."

Jack nods toward the door. "We'll have enough time to pick up Alain's drugged champagne from our cabana."

"I can't show up in this soaked caftan! I'll have to change." I sigh. "If illicit sex is the norm with these guys, why don't they hold their convention in Vegas or Amsterdam, where prostitution is legal?"

Jack guffaws. "When you're used to unbridled power, money, and privilege, what would be the fun in that?"

He's got a point.

7

Fringe Benefits

In addition to financial compensation, some companies offer "fringe benefits" universally or at the executive level as a recruitment, retainment, or motivation incentive. Examples are company swag, extra days off, a financial bonus (perhaps specified with terms but not necessarily), gift cards, free hotel stays, and even free airfare.

Fringe benefits may also be an unexpected award for a job well done.

If your company never promised you a fringe benefit—even worse, if it has been offered to others and not you—the message is clear:

Find a company that appreciates your skills and wants to reward you for them.

By the way, if a boss considers you a "fringe benefit," do whatever it takes to defend yourself. Then find a new job.

Better yet, find a good attorney.

Changed and armed with Alain's goodies, Jack and I head to the French banker's cabana. I've also brought two flutes.

I knock on Alain's door with a few minutes to spare. By now, I anticipate he'll be wearing only a robe.

He doesn't disappoint. To his credit, he's a handsome man: a strong nose, dark curly hair, and bedroom eyes. Like Mùchén, Alain is drowning out the ominous wind with music: in his case, Bridgette Bardot's *B.B.* album, from her mid-1960s heyday. The song, *Ne Me Laisse Pas L'Aimer*, is part croon and part pout.

Alain shimmies to the beat as he takes the bottle from me. He nods for me to follow him to the kitchen counter, where I leave his gift box. I'm about to take his towels to the bathroom, but he declares, *"Non, non! Nous ferons ça ensemble plus tard, Chérie!"*—his warning we're to end up together in the tub after a bit of bubbly.

Alain quickly unwraps the foil around the bottle's cork and is about to pop it when there's a knock on the door.

Like me, Alain is surprised. He motions for me to open it.

It's a woman:

Sabine DeBois.

At least Alain's robe is tied with a sash. But hers is left open displaying two generous breasts, a pierced belly button, a golden all-over tan, and a barely-there Brazilian: the same auburn shade as the hair on her head.

"Were you going to start the party without me?" Her purr reflects a thick French accent. "Unless *trois* is considered a crowd?"

Hmmm…

Alain's leer gets broader. His conquest is now doubly assured. "Not at all! *Entrez, mon ami.*"

I step aside to let her in. As I head out the door, he declares, "And you too, mademoiselle. We drink, we get cozy…we enjoy a *menage a trois. Oui, mon cheri?*"

Non, connard.

Suddenly, a quizzical look darkens his face. "*Sacrebleu!*"

Sabine cradles his face. "What is wrong, *mon ami?*"

"We have only two champagne flutes. One cannot sip the juice of God's best grape from *a fruit juice glass.*" Consternation etches Alain's face.

"Of course not, monsieur," I back up to the door. "Please start without me. I'll leave at once to collect another flute—"

"*Non, non!*" Alain looks at Sabine. "Perhaps you have some in your cabana?"

Adamantly, she shakes her head. "*Désolé, mais non.*"

There is a knock.

Again, Alain signals for me to answer it.

Jack stands at the door. He's holding two more champagne flutes.

Where the heck did he get them?

Jack points to me. "Forgive my intrusion. My colleague forgot this part of your delivery."

Sabine perks up. Jack may have foiled her ploy to get rid of me, but at the same time, she's been presented with a mouthwatering alternative. By now, she's drooling. You'd think Jack is a slab of Grade-A prime sirloin.

And with four glasses, it's now a real party.

To make it clear whom he covets, Alain puts his arm on the small of my back.

Jack sidles up to Sabine. She's not at all disappointed.

Finally, Alain gets to pop the bottle's cork. "Here's to the storm missing us," he toasts, then gulps down the contents of his glass, as does Sabine.

Like me, Jack feigns a sip. Then, by leaning into Sabine to stare lovingly into her eyes, he makes sure she misses his sleight-of-hand: draining his glass into the ice bucket.

Not to be outdone, Alain kisses me. I'm stunned, which is a good excuse to drop my flute on the floor. Our lip lock is long. In no time, he's dizzy enough to drape over me for support.

He doesn't see that Jack is carrying Sabine to his bed.

I follow Jack's lead, two-stepping Alain in the same direction. By the time I've got him bedside, Sabine is already curled up on one side of the mattress, naked. Jack helps me position Alain, who is also disrobed, to cradle her. As a final touch, Jack moves the ice bucket beside the bed and places the empty champagne bottle in it, neck down.

A search of Alain's cabana comes up empty of weapons, munitions, or anything that can prove he's part of the terrorist attack. Sabine's is also devoid of evidence. We leave her requested goodies—the champagne, extra towels, her gift box—and head out.

They'll wake up with hangovers and no recollection of what happened.

It'll be up to them to imagine the possibilities.

At seven, As promised, I show up on Claudio Cervantes' doorstep with a bag of raw shrimp, miniature storm lamps, a complimentary bottle of the drugged wine, and his gift box.

At the right time, Jack will show up with his extra towels.

The sound of traditional flamenco music comes from inside. A tap on the door garners the command, "*Entra, por favor!*"

The last thing I'd expect is that Claudio is blind. He stands behind the kitchen counter, holding a guide stick. Though he smiles, his dark glasses make it difficult for me to gauge the veracity of his affliction, which wasn't noted on his dossier.

After putting the gift box on the coffee table, I reply, "I have the shrimp." I speak in English to gauge his knowledge of the language.

"*Gracias, mi amor.* As you can see, the rice is already made." Claudio's accent is slight and Castellan in its cadence. He points at the stove, where a large wrought iron skillet is filled with yellow rice simmering with garlic, tomatoes, Spanish olives, peas, and red peppers. The scent of saffron—the spice that gives the rice its distinctive color— fills the air.

Stunned, I murmur, "Sir, if you've lost your sight, how did you prepare this meal?"

"It is the signature dish of my country. For generations, it has been handed down in our families. It is ingrained in every cell of my being." He beckons me. "Will you help me shell and clean *las camerones?*"

"Yes, of course."

I leave the door open so that Jack can follow me in, and then pray that, between the music, the storm, and the process of shelling and cleaning raw shrimp under running water will cover Jack's stealth.

As is the tradition, we create a broth with the shrimp shells to moisten the cooked rice. As the broth hits the hot skillet, the water sizzles, and a cloud of steam hits our faces. Claudio licks his lips and then grins.

The sound should have covered Jack's gentle footsteps. And yet, for a mere moment, Claudio looks directly at him. Aware of this, Jack stops, standing as still as a statue. In time, Claudio shrugs. "We must also scorch the rice at the bottom of the pan—but *uno pocito,*" he warns. "A bit of *vino blanco también.*"

When Claudio is satisfied that the meal is ready, Jack is tiptoeing to the door. His downward thumb tells me what I already know: Claudio isn't a viable suspect.

Before I can make an excuse to leave, Claudio insists that I join him in enjoying the fruits of our labor. "I have a perfect wine for such a feast." He points to a bottle of Peñas Aladas 2014 Gran Reserva. "Please do me the honor of opening and pouring it for us."

Leaving the drugged wine aside, I do as he asks.

"Perhaps your friend would also like to join us?" he adds.

I stutter, "My…what?"

Claudio chuckles. "The man who followed you in."

"But…I…"

"Señorita, I appreciate your indulging my need for… *cómo se dice en Inglés?* Ah, yes: 'comfort food.' If he is not a thief—I know this because my valuables are equipped with sensors that alert me. I would like to know why he and you need to search my cabana." He smiles. "At the very least, it should make for interesting dinner conversation."

I glance at Jack and nod.

He shrugs and then walks over to Claudio. "Señor Cervantes, my name is Jack Craig. Your concierge is my wife, Donna. We are special operatives sanctioned by our government, the United States, to work with the Tanzanian government to seek out terrorists embedded here for the banking event."

"*Dios mio!*" Claudio sighs. "But not surprising."

"Why do you say that?" I ask.

"Too many others assume that a blind man is also deaf. When I got on my flight to Tanzania from Paris, The flight attendant led me to a seat in front of two gentlemen and a woman. By the middle of the night, the cabin's lights are extinguished to facilitate travelers' attempts to sleep. Being blind, this does not affect me. The passengers behind me assumed otherwise. Though they talked in low voices, my ears overcompensate for what my eyes cannot see, and I was privy to their conversation. I found it disconcerting that they were discussing this resort and the location of each delegate's cabana— even more so when one of the men used the word 'extermination.' However, the other gentleman was insistent that the impact would be great if it were done, and I quote, 'during the opening day ceremony, since it will be live-streamed.'"

"Could you tell their country of origin by their accents?" Jack asks.

Claudio grimaces. "Each had a different accent. "The woman's was Slavic. One of the men is British. Another male is American. All spoke English. Perhaps it is the language they have in common."

"Have you reported your concerns to anyone else?" I ask.

Claudio shakes his head. "No. Frankly, I did not know who to trust."

He takes a step closer, close enough to reach out to me. He touches my face. Then, very gently, his hand roams over it. In time, he says, "I do now. Shall we eat, Señor and Señora Craig?"

Claudio is disappointed that we can only stay until our next concierge delivery. By then, we've made a big dent in his wonderful meal. "You'll find a gift box on your coffee table, compliments of the resort," I tell him. "We have also left two battery-operated lamps."

He chuckles. "The lamps are of no use for me. Feel free to take them with you."

As we walk to our cabana, Jack says, "At least you don't need yet another change of clothes. So, who's next?"

"The Japanese bankers. I'm to bring extra towels and do a bed turndown. Of course, I'll leave lamps too. The male's name is Hikaru Shimizu. The woman is Akira Gima. They arrived separately. According to her dossier, a concierge noted that she was distressed to learn her cabana was next to her countryman and asked to be moved. They rode in on different private jets, but too late for her to get a different cabana since the other attendees had already arrived."

"Do either Akira or Hikaru have asterisks by their names?"

"No, which will make it difficult for one of us to distract them."

"Perhaps we should deliver complimentary bottles of wine along with the towels and gift boxes," Jack suggests.

"It's worth a try."

I grab two bottles of the sedated wine and a corkscrew, which, in the worst-case scenario, will also serve as a weapon.

We head over to their cabanas, hoping they'll welcome a chance to get tipsy before the storm hits.

8

Onerous Contract

A contract that costs a company more to fulfill than what the company will receive in return is called an "onerous contract."

It is used in many countries. International regulators require such contracts to be disclosed on a company's balance sheet. However, the United States's system is known as "generally accepted accounting principles," or GAAP, and it does not consider an onerous contract a bad thing.

To use a relationship metaphor: if several of your friends swear that the guy who is eyeing you has a reputation for being bad news, take the hint:

You've got much more at stake than a walk of shame, so mind the GAAP!

Towels, wine, gift box, and lamps in hand, I knock on Hikaru's door first. No answer. So I knock again.

Still, no answer—

But I see movement through the cabana's floor-to-ceiling glass window.

From his dossier photo, it's Hikaru. He hesitates. But then he looks behind him—

At a woman—short, slim, dark-haired, also in a bathrobe—who runs and hides behind the galley kitchen's counter.

By the time Hikaru turns to face me, I've turned my head skyward as if gauging the storm's fury.

He comes to the door. Smiling, I bow slightly, "Sorry to disturb you, sir, but the manager insists I present these battery-operated lamps, our welcome gift box, and this fine wine, which he hopes will calm your nerves during the storm. May I come in?" I ask.

Hikaru pauses but then steps aside.

Upon entering, I bow. "I shall leave the items there," I say, pointing to the kitchen counter.

I walk over to it. "But before I do, I'll open the wine for you. The manager insists we do so to give this fine cabernet a chance to breathe before you sip." I hold up the corkscrew. Still chatting gayly. I add," By the way, the best glass to sip from are the ones in this lower cabinet—"

I move behind the counter—

Almost stepping on Akira.

She crawls backward against the refrigerator. Then, putting her hands over her face, she exclaims, "Please! Do not tell anyone that you saw me here! I don't wish to be disgraced."

"Disgraced?…But why?" I glare at Hikaru. "Did he coerce you into this…this compromising position?"

"*No!* What I mean to say is…" Akira is trembling so hard that she can't speak.

Hikaru declares, "We are married!"

"*Married?*" Shocked, I put the bottle on the counter. "But… Mademoiselle Gima…that is, Madame Gima…or Madame *Shimizu*…You made a big fuss about changing to another cabana not to be next to Monsieur Shimizu!"

Akira is hysterical. Why is that?

The only advantage to this is that Jack can slip past him into the cabana's bedroom.

So now, it's up to me to keep them occupied until he can slip out again. No problem there since I already find their shenanigans quite intriguing.

I sigh. "Sir and madame, why the charade?"

"Because no one must know we are man and wife," Hikaru explains.

"Why is that?" I ask.

Tears roll down Ikira's cheeks. "Not only will I shame myself, I'll shame my bank. And I will also shame my husband and his bank. "

"Some call it Japan's 'rice paper ceiling,'" Hikaru adds. "Despite our president's goal of encouraging our corporations to see women as men's equals in the work-force, they are paid less than men even if given the same job. Neither are they promoted at the same rate."

"And yet, Akira, somehow you beat the system," I point out. "Otherwise, you wouldn't be here representing your bank."

Hikaru goes to her side. "Because her skills as an economist are second to none. Akira was first in our class at university. Her bank was smart enough to recognize this—to the foolishness and detriment of mine." He reaches down to give his wife a helping hand.

She takes it. Looking at me, she implores, "Neither of our employers knows we are married. Were they to find out, we would be terminated. And no other Japanese bank would hire us."

"With your reputation as an economist, you'd be hired immediately by any bank in the world, either together or separately," I venture.

"That is true," Akira admits. "But it would mean uprooting our children, who are attended to by Hikaru's mother as if they are her own. I mean that figuratively and literally since they bear his surname."

"I am sorry for you and for them. Please understand I have no intention of mentioning what you've told me to anyone. I will hold onto your secret, always."

The couple's relief is expressed with murmurs of "Ariosto" and deep bows—

Long enough for Jack to slip away.

So that he can search Akira's room too, I open the cabernet, take two glasses from the cabinet, and pour their wine. Handing each a glass, I proclaim: "Here is to your success, both at home and abroad."

Akira insists, "You must also share in our toast."

I'm tempted, but then I remember the sleeping sedative in the wine. "No, no! It is against the resort's policy. I must finish my rounds now. Have a comfortable evening."

I back out of the room, bowing.

When I get back to our cabana, Jack is already there. "Nothing that points to sabotage," he assures me. "And, frankly, I'm glad it isn't them."

"Me too," I admit, "although when I heard Hikaru speak with an impeccable British accent, I realized that Claudio's eavesdropping would not have detected him as a target."

"As did Akira," Jack points out. "I assume they were educated in the UK."

"At least now we've ruled them out," I reply. I check the electronic pad for our next target. "A bit of good news: this attendee's request is for fresh fruit juice, and there are no asterisks beside it. He's Canadian. Blaine Wentworth, mid-forties. Canada is also this year's official host country. It is a rotating position among all countries' delegates. As such, Blaine sets the event's agenda based on delegates' votes. From his dossier, he's been his country's representative for the past decade, but this is the first year he's taken on the lead role."

"This works in his favor on both counts. It gives credence to his clean bill of health unless he's been compromised. In that case, he's the perfect Trojan horse," Jack points out. "Claudio identified one of our three prime targets as a native-English speaker from America. Perhaps he mistook the accent for American when it was Canadian."

"Doubtful. Considering Claudio's handicap, I'd assume his ear is sharply attuned to accents."

Jack concedes with a sigh. "We'll know soon enough. The trick for you is to get this Blaine Wentworth guy to drink it before you leave so we can search his place together and get out quickly."

"I'll do my best, but no guarantees," I warn him. "Fingers crossed Blaine is as harmless and as forthcoming as Claudio."

I knock on Blaine Wentworth's door promptly at seven, bearing the usual drop-off items with the addition of a small metal crate of six bottles of freshly squeezed—and now drugged—pineapple juice. From inside, someone yells, "Come in!"

I enter a silent, pitch-dark room. The windows' shutters are closed but can't block out the storm's howling winds.

Creepy.

In time, my eyes make out a flickering light in the farthest corner of the room. A candle, perhaps set on the floor?

Things are getting creepier…

"You have my juice." The voice, though lighthearted, has a fevered singsong pitch. "Come closer, pretty lady! I'm so, so thirsty!"

My instincts force a smile onto my lips. I hold my arm steady so the juice bottles don't rattle in their metal carrier. The thirty or so feet between me and the face reflected in the candle's light suddenly seem much too close—

Especially now that it illuminates the barrel of a gun.

With each step, I scan the room for possible weapons. Wentworth sits on the wall flanking the kitchen galley. Should I lunge toward the counter in search of a weapon —knife, cleaver, even a pan to use as a shield, whatever— I'd be showing my hand and forcing his.

And so I move forward slowly, as if I don't have a care in the world while feigning obliviousness and utmost politeness.

"My, my, you're pretty! And what gifts do you bring me?"

"The pineapple juice you requested. Squeezed fresh, by me, and the resort's welcome gift box."

"The juice…It seems like a million years ago since I ordered it." Wentworth's voice trails off. Seeing the gift box, he giggles. "And she comes bearing gifts, too! As apropos as it is ironic." He shrugs. "Since we're all going to die anyway, better sooner than later."

By now, I'm standing directly in front of him. "Sir, I know you're worried about the storm. As are all of us. But we're on high ground. Island life teaches us to wait it out—"

Now he's cackling like a deranged clown—

And pointing the gun directly at me. "'Island life?' Seriously, *Mrs. Craig?*"

Hearing my name, I almost drop the crate.

"Pardon me?"

He cocks the gun. "Take a seat. That way, there's less of a chance your dead body will fall on me when I blow your head off."

"Were you to blow it off, you'd have nothing to worry

about since the force of the blast would propel me backward."

He takes that in with a resigned frown. "I was never that great at science."

"That's okay. I'm not much of a shrink, but considering our dilemma here, I'll give psychoanalysis a go. Tell me: why do you feel the need to shoot me in the first place?"

"Because you're here to stop them." His psychotic bravado has been replaced by fear.

"How do you know about the 'them' of whom you speak?"

"Because, as this year's host country, I'm the one who arranged for them to get here and to pass themselves off as the rest of us: we, the masters and mistresses of high finance!"

"*You?*... But... How? Why?"

"Because I believed in what they said was their cause."

"And what is that?"

"The annihilation of a world economy in which the rich get richer while hundreds of millions of others—*whole nations*—are starving and left to die in abject poverty!" Blaine grabs my arm and pulls me closer. "Don't you get it? This is one big circle jerk! A big farce! Well, I'm through closing my eyes to it! I'm through pretending that anyone cares! I'm through—"

"You're through pretending that you did something noble. You're scared because you played into their hands, and now you realize you screwed up. But no, you haven't.

There's still time to stop the slaughter. Tell me who 'they' are before it begins. Blaine, seriously—"

"You don't get it! This is already happening! *And they control you too!*"

Blaine raises the gun—

And puts it in his mouth—

Just as a crash of thunder echoes the gunshot that takes his life.

A bolt of lightning illuminates the hole that was once his face before the explosion cratered his head.

The tumultuous storm drowns out the screams—

My screams—

Which don't stop until Jack takes me in his arms as if shielding me against some unknown chaos that is still to come.

"Maybe you should skip this next target search," Jack suggests. "You know, get your bearings."

"I can't! You heard Blaine. Time is of the essence!" At least now I've quit shaking. We roam through Blaine's cabana, opening drawers, cupboards, and closets, looking under the bed, raising carpets for hidden hatches or loose floorboards, and tapping walls for secret cubbies.

And yet, we find nothing. No weapons. No munitions. No notes with an agenda for the looming disaster or names of accomplices.

Not even a farewell to loved ones.

Before taking our leave, we wrap his body in a carpet.

How many more will we leave behind us?

Worse yet, will ours be left in this godforsaken place, this once-considered paradise that is now a living hell?

When we get back to our cabana, Jack takes me straight to the bathroom and strips me down, then puts me in the shower and gets in, too, holding me tight.

As we stand under the water, the blowback from Blaine's blood and skull isn't the only thing to wash away:

I must shake off the dread that Jack and I are doomed here;

That we'll never see our children again. And that, if what Blaine said is true, weather-permitting—that some army of terrorists will soon descend on us.

But no. I refuse to die here.

I'll fight like hell until this is over.

Then I remember my next two stops are the cabanas where the British bankers reside.

Claudio's warning about overhearing the British saboteur on the plane comes to mind. Should I dread that one, or both, will be revealed as terrorists?

No. I welcome it.

GAME. ON.

I shut off the water. "Shall we get on to our next targets?" Grabbing two towels, I toss one to Jack.

He catches it with a single hand. "Who are they?"

I take the electronic device from its hiding place. "In truth, there are two: the British Bankers."

"Bingo," Jack declares. "One of them has got to be the British accent Claudio heard on the plane. What are their concierge requests?"

"Just one—this large portfolio." As I pick it up, I

chastise myself for not having the time to open its wax seal, see if it held coded orders to the imminent massacre, and then reheat the seal again.

Ah, well. So many tasks, so little time. "We're late, so let's get this show on the road."

9

For a Song

In financial dealings, when someone offers something "for a song," they're implying that you're getting a deal—

That is, a reduction in the asset's cost.

Should you believe them?

Well, that depends. Are you playing with your money or that of others?

Note of caution: if the asset doesn't come with a certified appraisal, you may want to get one.

Let's face it: there's nothing worse than finding out you got ripped off because you were silly enough to buy into someone else's lie.

When it comes to your investments, the last thing you want to do is sing the blues.

"You're late, dearie." Sir Colin Hodgson-Payne is peeved that I'm five minutes late with the folio.

Besides Sir Colin's off-putting tone, he adds insult to injury by scrutinizing me through a monocle. Seriously? Do people wear those things in this day and age?

Then I notice that his cohort, the Right Honorable Reginald Smythe-Brantley, is wearing a bicorne hat: the spitting image of the one Admiral Nelson wore at the Battle of Trafalgar.

Suddenly, I feel as if I've walked into a costume party. If they're into cosplay, I hope it doesn't include gags, whips, and fetishwear that's a bit more revealing.

Ah, heck—I hope I haven't been summoned to take on the role of The Lusty Wench!

Sir Colin taps the portfolio in my hand. "May I?"

"By all means." I hand it to him.

He opens it. Suddenly, he frowns. "Oh, balderdash, Reggie! Your secretary sent the wrong ditty!"

Smythe-Brantley takes the portfolio. His verification comes with a groan. "A *trio?* Good God! Where will we get a soprano?"

Suddenly, their eyes rake over me.

Sir Colin pulls a harmonica from his vest pocket and plays a note: C. Then he asks, "Can you sing that?"

I accommodate.

He glances over at Reggie, who nods. "It'll do."

Now I'm intrigued. "What will do, pray tell?"

"How familiar are you with Gilbert and Sullivan's *HMS Pinafore?*" Sir Colin asks.

They have their answer when I respond:

> *Never mind the why and wherefore,*
> *Love can level ranks, and therefore*

I admit the jurisdiction;
Ably have you played your part;
You have carried firm conviction
To my hesitating heart.

I have yet one more reason to thank Mrs. Moon, my junior-year chorus teacher, for insisting that our class tackle Gilbert & Sullivan.

Colin chuckles. "Jolly good, eh, Reg? I'd say we've found our 'Josephine!'" He waves a hundred-pound note in front of my nose. "We shall make the task worth your while."

I'll say! I snatch it out of his hand. "In the key of B, gentlemen."

Colin slaps Reggie's chest. "You'll be Captain, eh? And I'll be Sir Joseph."

He walks over to the cabana's grand piano, finds the proper key, and off we go:

Reggie as Captain:
Never mind the why and wherefore,
Love can level ranks, and therefore,
Though his lordship's station's mighty,
Though stupendous be his brain,
Though her tastes are mean and flighty
And her fortune poor and plain...

Out of the corner of my eye, I see Jack inching his way through the front door. Since Reggie and Colin have their backs to it and are singing so loudly and, albeit, resolutely—one as a bass, the other a baritone—they don't see Jack sneak in, let alone make his way into Reggie's bedroom.

During the second stanza, I interject my solo line ("*…For a gallant captain's daughter…*") between Colin's and Reggie's calls and responses, and then my next one ("*And a tar who ploughs the water!…*") before joining their chorus:

> *Let the air with joy be laden,*
> *Rend with songs the air above,*
> *For the union of a maiden*
> *With the man who owns her love!*

Jack makes it out the door as our melded voices crescendo in sustained harmony for the finale.

If only all covert ops ended as beautifully.

Colin and Reggie insist on several encores. I stick it out. This should give Jack the necessary time to search Reggie's cabana.

Admittedly, another ton note from Colin makes it easy to say yes.

They also extend an open invitation to join their Mayfair-based operatic society whence my travels take me to London.

How can I say no?

As for the rest of my evening, I realize this is just the entr'acte.

This mission is no comedy. Tragedy must be avoided at all costs.

~

Jack is waiting for me at our cabana. "Both the Brits were clean as a whistle. And speaking of which: *wow*! Could they carry a tune, or what?" He taps my nose. "And so could you, my little showstopper! Gilbert and Sullivan? Who knew?"

"I'm a woman of many talents," I remind him. "And next up is—" I glance at the dossier pad—"the two German bankers, Hans Felder and Gunther Koehl.

Along with the usual items, Jack delivers their request for a case of their favorite German beer, Schorschbräu Schorschbock 57. He's also taken two hefty beer steins. What makes these special is that they are lined with the sleeping sedative.

As I round the corner to Gunther's cabana, I hear voices singing a classic Teutonic song. You know, the typical stuff that brings tears to the eyes of half-soused ex-pats already nostalgic and homesick for their homeland. Hans and Gunther have imbibed heartily because they're rowdy and off-key. My husband's enthusiastic baritone is the only voice that isn't slurring from the drugged drinks.

I give it a few more minutes: just long enough for the enthusiasm in their voices to die out completely. In time, only their snores can be heard. I enter and search Gunther's cabana. His pictures are the kind you'd find on a true blue family man's photo feed: his wife and kids dressed in their Sunday best, or family snapshots of camping and fishing trips. He also coaches one boy's soccer team.

My search of his room reinforces his innocence. I leave a battery-operated lamp and the towels.

In the meantime, Jack searches Hans' cabana. Whereas Hans, who is single, has succeeded in convincing a few women to pose in compromising positions. No crime there.

And no bombs.

We head back to our cabana to prep for our next search.

~

Jack waits until we're inside and our travel tradecraft shows our cabana is still secure before asking, "Who's left?"

I check the electronic dossiers. "Oh, this is just dandy," I mutter. "It's Gretta Ullman! She's one of the event's coordinators. Swiss."

"I take it there's no double asterisk by her name."

"None, so you're off the hook for sexcapades." Frankly, I'm relieved. "The orders are to drop fresh towels. You'll leave lamps too—and, of course, the resort's gift box. You're also to pick up a loaded food cart. There will be instructions on where to deliver it and when." I sigh. "Jack, I don't know how I'll get you in there."

"While you put the towels in her bathroom and search her room, I'll arrive with a free bottle of wine," Jack suggests.

I shrug. "I guess it's as good a plan as any. Let's get moving."

~

Jack arrives at Gretta's room promptly at seven-thirty. To stagger our appearances, I keep out of view on her cabana's veranda.

When Jack knocks, Gretta is on the resort's house phone. She barks, "Come in!"

After dropping the resort's welcome items on her coffee table, he leaves the door open for me. Though he waits patiently for her to address him, she paces the room restlessly. "You don't think I know what happens at those so-called 'poker games?' You're a fool, Phillip, for allowing it! There's no way they'll get away with it! Should word get out, we'll be ruined!"

I deduce she's talking to her American counterpart running the event. Claudio heard a woman with an accent. Could it have been hers? Granted, it is Swedish, not Slavic…

When she has her back to the door, I slip in, towels in hand, and make my way through the bedroom to the bathroom. I do a quick sweep of the room. I check the drawers and under the bed. I check floors, walls, and then the closet, where Gretta's clothes are lined up on hangers. Her suitcases are empty.

By now, Jack has positioned himself to block Gretta's view of me. Not that it matters. Purposefully, she has her back to him as she hisses, "If the US delegation pulls that stunt, they can ruin the conference! It word should ever get out…"

I can't see why, but she's stopped talking for some reason. Then I hear her say to Jack, "Yes, thank you for the storm lamps and these other things. You can leave with that cart over there …No, please, do not open the bottle! I don't drink. Yes, go on, Paul…*No!* I mean what I say—"

As Jack passes the bedroom window, he gives me the high sign to speed it up.

Nothing looks suspicious.

I hurry to the bathroom but find no weaponry, let alone anything that bangs, ticks, or blows up.

I'm just going out when I hear her coming into the bedroom. She's still on the phone.

I scoop up the dirty towels on the floor and walk out whistling.

She stares at me.

I stop whistling to ask, "Other than towels, is there anything else I may bring you, madam?"

Warily, she asks, "When did you get in here? Did you overhear my conversation?"

"No, madam! I…I came in with the other concierge. Because of the storm, we've been ordered to stay in pairs to facilitate the guests' wishes as quickly as possible."

For some reason, this relieves her. She pats my hand. "It's an excellent policy. Keep him by your side."

What the heck does she mean by that?

My skin crawls, and I don't know why.

I can't run out of here quickly enough.

When we're back in our cabana, Jack asks, "Are we seeing a pattern here?"

"If you mean that we have no suspects, heck yes! And it concerns me," I admit.

"You and me both!" He smacks the wall, frustrated. "I just don't get it."

I throw this out: "Maybe our adversary isn't here yet."

"We know at least three of them were on Claudio's plane: a Slavic woman, a British man, and an American male," Jack reminds me. "Considering their targets are just twenty-three people who will be sitting ducks in that glass bowl up there"—he points to the resort's peak-cresting conference room—"it's feasible that they could carry out the threat on their own."

"Trust me, neither Reggie nor Colin is our Brit. And while Hikaru's accent is spot-on, I don't believe he was faking his love for Akira," I reply. "At the same time, I don't believe Claudio mistook the accents he'd heard."

"From what I heard, I couldn't agree more." He shrugs. "Okay, where are we off to now?"

"The American bankers have yet to be vetted."

"What do we know about them?"

I hand him the electronic pad so that Jack can scan their dossiers. "In a nutshell: there are three of them," I point out. "Two are the US bank representatives Howard Krebs and Edward Randall Morton the Third. According to our concierge service orders, they're in a poker game with the other coordinator—Phillip Warburton—in his cabana." I look at the clock. "I'm supposed to deliver snacks, wine, and drinks in twenty minutes." I point to the refrigerated cart Emmanuel gave me earlier today—to my mind, a million years ago. It holds sandwiches on one side, dips and chips on another, and a beautiful chocolate cake between them.

"Was a bed turn-down requested?" Jack asks.

"Yes."

He frowns. "Did the request come with asterisks?"

"Thankfully, no."

Relief eases Jack's grimace. "By now, Phillip and Randall will have left their cabanas. Let's take the cart. While you make the delivery, I'll search their places."

Jack takes my hand, and away we go.

10

Alpha

I*f an investment strategy reaps an "excess return" or an "abnormal rate of return" when compared to what is needed to hit its benchmark (adjusted for risk), it is praised as being "Alpha."*

This term can also describe men who show an abnormal rate of machismo.

Some women are attracted to such men.

However, there is one annoying and, sadly, consistent trait these males share: their expectations of your investment of time and effort in them may far exceed what you get in return.

So ask yourself: when adjusted for any risk—be that of his taking you for granted, or viewing women as benchmarks that need to be hit upon and audaciously doing so hitting on either in front of you or behind your back—is he still worth it?

An alternate investment strategy: check out your Beta options.

You'll find them tremendously well-adjusted. Ergo, a better investment of your time and your heart.

We enter Randall's cabana first, leaving his gift box and the event planners' welcome note where he can't miss it: on the table next to the door. The place is pristine. I warn Jack: "If you move anything, return it exactly as you found it."

"Aye, aye, captain!" To reinforce this vow, he salutes—

But when he swings his hand out, he knocks over a large vase filled with Birds of Paradise. It topples off the counter—

And crashes onto the kitchen's clay tile floor.

"Not part of the game plan, sir," I growl. Grabbing a broom and dustpan from the closet, I sweep up the vase's shards and drop them on the cart's bottom shelf while Jack picks up the flowers. After tossing them off the cabana's verandah, he takes one of the new towels we'd brought in as part of our cover and mops up the spillage.

The rest of Randall's suite is just as pristine. Expecting better weather, he's brought several Panama hats, cravats, Ferragamo vests, Abercrombie sweaters, Gucci Bermuda shorts, and Oxford shirts from Saville Row's Drake's.

As for any weaponry, we find *nada.*

Next, we go to Howard's cabana. The place is in total disarray. "Either it's been tossed by our adversary, or he's just one big slob," I mutter as I kick aside the bedroom's throw pillows. A stash of hardcore porn magazine is beneath them.

I shudder at their covers.

A computer has been left on his messy bed beside a soiled washcloth. I opened it to find he'd been watching a video before taking off to his meeting. Gobsmacked, I watch it: amateur and grainy, a man rapes a struggling woman—in truth, barely a teenager—who is blindfolded, ball-gagged, and tied to the bedposts—

Before snuffing her out.

Jack hears my gasp. Looking over my shoulder, he watches as I play it for him.

When it ends, his eyes are still riveted on the screen. He presses the replay button and watches it again.

"See the man garroting her? He's the guy staying in this cabana!"

I take a closer look. Jack is right: it's the man in Howard's dossier.

"You are not going into that poker game!" Jack declares.

"But I have to! Otherwise, how will we search Phillip's cabana?"

"I'll deliver the cart," he insists. Once I'm inside, I'll figure out a way to get them to drink the drugged wine and do the search myself."

I shake my head. "We both know I'd be the best diversion."

"No way, Don! If anything happens, you'll be outnumbered three to one. I can't let you do it. And besides, with what we've discovered through all the other searches, it may be a moot point. So far, only one of these attendees has been complicit in the threat: Blaine Wentworth, who openly admitted it before he killed himself. And let's not forget that he almost killed you too."

"Let's also not forget that one of our targets happens

to be an American male. If that's the case, more than likely he's one of those three men," I insist. "Jack, I have to be the bait whether you like it or not. And besides, Howard wouldn't show that side of himself to the others. Even one illegal indiscretion in front of strangers who have too much to lose and they'd ostracize him—or worse yet, turn him in. They wouldn't want the guilt by association."

Jack scowls as he thinks this through. Finally, he hands me a bottle of the drugged wine and mutters, "Insist that the resort's manager requests they try the wine with his compliments. If anything goes wrong, yell. I'll be right outside."

I know he's unhappy with this compromise, but the only way to vet Phillip is to search his room.

I head out first with the cart.

The men's laughter is loud enough to drown out the squall whipping around us. I have to knock twice to get someone's attention.

Phillip Burton finally opens the door. "Ah, a beauty comes bearing treats!"

I glance over his shoulder. The others sit around a table. They hold playing cards. A pile of bills from different countries and various denominations sits dead center on the table.

Phillip stands aside so that I can push the cart toward the open kitchen.

But then he shuts the door. As the deadbolt lock clicks, my heart jolts.

"Who won this hand again?" Phillip asks.

"You," Randall declares. "So you get to go first with her."

With her.

With me.

All three men are standing now. In a few strides, they're too close for comfort.

And yet, I keep a smile on my face. "I've also brought something extraordinary for you, compliments of the resort's owner." I hold up the bottle of wine. I reach for the corkscrew—

Only to have Howard grab my wrist. "That's okay, sugar pie. Our libations are covered." He holds a beer in his other hand. "Instead, why don't you join us?"

"Against the rules, I'm afraid." I jerk free of his grasp.

"That's not what I hear." Randall chuckles. To prove he knows the score, he tweaks my nipple. "More than a mouthful, for sure." When he buries his head in my breasts, the other men roar with laughter.

Phillip, now directly behind me, grabs me by the waist and shoves me against the cart until I'm bent over it. "Guess what's for dessert, guys?"

I feel his hard-on. But when he backs away to unbuckle his belt, I jab the corkscrew into his side and twist it.

His howl rocks the room. Although he staggers away shrieking, Howard bolts toward me. He holds a Taser in his hand. He jabs, but I dodge it. When he comes at me again, I kick him in the groin, and he drops it on the floor. I grab the Taser and zap him with it. The shock is strong enough that he is thrown backward into a wall.

Just as he drops to the floor, convulsing, Randall punches me in the gut.

I double over at the base of the cart.

When he crouches to pick me up, I reach into the cart's bottom shelf for something—anything—that I can use as a weapon.

Randall rises with me in his arms. He's striding to the bedroom we hear a crash:

One of the verandah rocking crashes through the cabana's glass wall.

Instinctively, Randall looks over—

And that's when I shove the ragged ceramic shard from the vase into his jugular.

Randall stops, gasps, and drops to his knees.

He's still holding me when he falls face down.

My head hits the floor, and I black out.

The ice against my forehead shocks me back to consciousness.

Though my eyes are blurry, I can make out Jack's face, concern etched on his forehead, drawing his lips downward into a frown.

My voice comes out as a croak: "What happened?"

"I threw the chair through the window to save you, but you'd already saved yourself."

"*What?...*what do you mean?" I try to sit up, but I'm still woozy.

"Let's just say you pulled a triple-whammy."

"Come again?"

"Just look around. Your attackers are dead." He points to Phillip, who is lying on his side in a pool of blood. "You stuck the corkscrew into his gut." Then he nods toward Howard. "When you Tased him, he had a fatal heart attack."

"What happened to Randall?"

Jack points in the direction of the kitchen. "I broke in just as you pierced Randalls's jugular. He dropped you on your head, which is why you passed out."

At the thought of it, my head pounds. And yet, I manage to ask, "I take it you searched the cabana?"

"Yep—and no sign of any terrorists' toys." Jack shrugs. "On the upside, with all of these now dearly departed bankers, the saboteurs will wreak less havoc."

"Hardy har har. What time is it now?"

"Almost midnight," Jack replies. "We have just one more delivery of towels to make. It's the Swedish banker, Oskar Surbeck."

"Thank goodness! Let me guess: he requested extra towels with asterisks."

"Unfortunately, yes."

Though I'm still woozy, I stand up. "Then he'll be expecting a massage and all that implies. We'll have to go back to our cabana for massage oil."

"No, we don't. Phillip and his buddy hoarded the stuff for their unsuspecting victims." Jack holds up a bottle. With crossed fingers, he adds, "Here's hoping that Oskar spent his university years in the UK and that he speaks with a British accent so that we finally get our man and we can end this vacation on a high note."

Wishful thinking on his part. Still, it earns him a kiss.

11

Straddle

The finance term "straddle" describes a "neutral options strategy"—that is, one that involves simultaneously buying both a "call option" and a "put option."

Since these options have the opposite effect, you may wonder, "Why would one do such a thing?"

To an outsider, it would raise the question: "Does this idiot know what she's doing?"

Indeed, she does. Her call option allows her a certain amount of time to place a stock order at a price lower than its current rate. Should it drop to that price, she wins! On the other hand, her put order is a contract giving her the right—but not the obligation—to sell, or sell short, a specified amount of the same security at a predetermined price within a specified time frame.

In other words, by doing both, she's hedging her bets.

It's precisely what you did when you half-heartedly accept a date with one guy in case the other guy you hoped would call leaves you hanging. Either way, you aren't sitting at home waiting for the phone to ring.

As commanded, I knock twice on Oskar's cabana door at exactly five-thirty. Even over the roiling squall hovering offshore, Classical music assaults my ears. I recognize it as Rachmaninoff's *Prelude in C-Sharp Minor*.

No one answers my double rap. The next time, I knock harder, and the door creaks open. I declare, "Hello?"

A male voice booms, "In the tub."

I leave the door open so that Jack can follow me inside. I head in its direction. As I do, I pass his bedroom. On the nightstand is a bracelet:

The one Tisa was wearing.

A chill tingles my spine. *Oskar Surbeck killed her and took it as a trophy.*

When we found Tisa's body, I hadn't noticed she wasn't wearing it. Stupid me—I hadn't mentioned it to CCI Salum, either.

"This isn't a big place, so that you couldn't have gotten lost." The irritation in his voice is ominous.

I slip the bracelet into the pocket of my caftan, and then I hurry to the bathroom.

I'd guess him to be around my age. Admittedly, he's easy on the eye. Oscar's blond hair is damp and slicked back. Though seated in bathwater, he's tall enough that his chiseled pecs are high above the deep tub's blanket of glistening bubbles.

Oskar nods toward the heated towel rack. "Put them there, my dear." His English has a soft German lilt. "Then I'd appreciate it if you'd scrub my back." He points to a long-armed boar-bristle brush. To accommodate, he sits straight up in the tub. "The soap is there." He points to the resort's signature bar, which is scented with plumeria grown on the island.

I take the soap, rub it against the brush, and gently cleanse his back.

"You're being much too delicate," He admonishes. "Harder, please."

I scrub harder: across his shoulders, down his spine, then to the left of his back, and then the right.

"Ah...yes! *Wonderful!*" The music is reaching a crescendo. But it, nor the storm, competes with his commands.

"It is indeed, sir." Does he notice the catch in my throat? If so, maybe he'll take it for my subservience—

Which will last only as long as it takes Jack to find evidence of Oskar's role in our mission.

"You may stop now." Oskar stands up and turns around.

I'm now face-to-face with *der schniedelshaft*—fully erect, I might add. "Surely you've heard the saying, "One good turn deserves another. I shall pamper you now."

Um...

No.

Before I know it, he takes the scrub brush from my hand.

When I reach over the side to retrieve it, he smacks my bum—*hard*—with the back of the brush. "Stand, please." His command is menacing.

I do as he asks.

"Now, disrobe."

"But…sir…"

Your pretense toward modesty is endearing but not necessary. If you must play coy, it shall be by my rules, of which one is supreme: 'cleanliness is next to godliness.' That said, I plan on scrubbing you within an inch of your life and then ravishing you."

"Sir…I—"

With both hands, he rips the caftan from my body.

Tisa's bracelet falls out of the garment's pocket and rolls on the floor before smacking against the bathroom's tile wall with a loud enough clang.

Oskar stares at it and then at me.

Before I can move, he grabs me by the shoulders and shoves me down into the water, face down.

Flailing, I fight him off, but his grasp is too firm. I hear him laughing.

I reach out to grab something—anything—

Something floats by my hand: I feel the brush's bristles.

I grasp it tightly, right below its head. Then, backhanded, I jab with all my might.

Oskar howls. Best yet, he lets go of my neck.

Gagging and coughing, I rise from the tub. When I focus my eyes, I realize I've stabbed him in the eye. A smear of soap marks his path to where he slipped before toppling backward and cracking his head against the tiled floor.

His head is haloed in blood.

Jack runs to the door but stops at its threshold. Scanning the situation, he murmurs, "Did he confess to being one of the bad guys?"

"He didn't have to." I pick up Tisa's bracelet and toss it to him. "He had this on his nightstand. A trophy, I guess. I took it as evidence. It fell out of my pocket when he ripped off my caftan."

Jack whistles. "I don't even want to think of what he'd have done to you."

"Let's don't then." Standing over the tub, I squeeze excess water out of the caftan. "I can't believe Oskar's sole indiscretion was rape and murder. Tell me you found something that also ties him to our mission."

"Sorry, hon. Nothing." Jack pats my shoulder. "Who's next on the list?"

I sigh. "Well, at least we've already taken care of one of them— Xiãng—which leaves us Rufus and Yulia."

Jack frowns. "You say Yulia was on the yacht, but I can't place her face."

"That's because she disappeared into the galley when the other women surrounded you."

Can he hear the contempt in my voice? If so, too bad since she's the only person who fits Claudio's description of the female Slavic voice.

Yulia.

"We can save them for tomorrow," Jack declares. "I'll need a good night's sleep for… Well, for tomorrow's task."

I'm relieved to hear him say that. I, too, would like to have one good night's sleep in my husband's arms before he has to make his move.

On three beautiful women.

I'm sure they won't make it difficult for him.

I shrug. "If that's the case, our final target for the

night is the other Chinese banker, Hu Gang. He wants extra towels—and yes, there's a double asterisk."

"What if he doesn't offer you a drink?" Jack asks.

"I'll think of some reason for him to open his mouth and say 'Ah.'"

Jack frowns. He knows my jokes are just my defense mechanism to cover for the anxiety of my sparrow role.

Tonight is no laughing matter.

This second honeymoon has gone to hell in a handcart.

12

Hyperinflation

This term describes rapid, excessive, and out-of-control general price increases in an economy. While inflation measures the pace of rising prices for goods and services, hyperinflation typically measures more than 50 percent per month.

Yikes! Tell me that doesn't hurt!

Hyperinflation is not a new term. Whereas it is first mentioned in writing in C. Bresciani-Turroni's 1931 Italian economics tome bemoaning Germany's hyperinflation after The Great War, it was evidenced as far back as Third Century Rome:

Proof that men's greediness can ruin things for everyone, including the ladies.

And, metaphorically speaking, especially where it counts most.

Pushing my cart with one hand and wrangling my umbrella in this waling rain storm, I go to Hu Gang's cabana.

Jack is not far behind. I wait until he's positioned behind the support wall separating the living area from the bedroom.

It is a while before Gang answers my door. When he does, Jack ducks behind the wall.

Gang is the antithesis of Mùchén: slight, with a muscular build.

"Bummer, doll! Sorry, but I got a better offer, so you're off the hook." Gang nods toward the bedroom.

His All-American surfer-dude Kenergy and his Stanford class ring call him out as American-born Chinese, which is unexpected but a smart move for any Chinese-based bank that wants insights into how a competing global superpower thinks regarding its investment strategy.

As unprepared as I am for this revelation, the next one leaves me just as slack-jawed:

Gang has already got company. A bikini-clad woman is strolling toward the bedroom:

But then Gang closes the door, so I can't see who it is.

Quickly, I put my foot in the doorway. Through my excruciating pain, I stutter, "But… Don't you want more fresh towels and the resort's welcome gift box? I also have a portable battery-operated lamp—and a bottle of our Special Reserve cabernet!" I hold up the bottle for Gang to see.

He hesitates. Still, he opens the door wide enough to take the towels and the gift box.

Darn it, the woman is nowhere in sight.

Perusing the wine's label, he sneers, "*What?* Are you kidding me? This stuff is mediocre swill! I should know.

My bank finances this winery." Noting my shock, he sighs. "Look, sugar pie, the truth is that three's company but four's a crowd——"

"The saying is 'two's company, *three's* a crowd," I counter.

"*Whatever.*" Gang rolls his eyes. "But seriously——*no, buts.*" To make his point, he tilts his head to take a look at my backside. He must like what he sees because he sighs. He reaches into his pocket and adds, "So that you don't feel you've wasted your time, here's a little something for being such a good sport." After taking the lamp from one of my hands, he shoves something into it.

I look down to find Benjamin Franklin's grimace staring up at me.

Well, I'm certainly not turning down a hundo.

I'm just about to say thanks when he shuts the door. Darn it!

I look over at Jack. His face has lost all its color.

"You look like you've seen a ghost," I say.

"It's not that. It's just that… Some vacation, eh?" He lowers his head, then rubs the weariness from his eyes. "Look, Don, Gang is the kind of guy who kicks his company out of his bed when he's done. One of us should get a good night's sleep. It might as well be you." He points to his umbrella. "I'll stay behind and act the gentleman."

I'm not going to argue. Instead, I hand him the wine.

Just then, we hear a roar above us, even louder than the storm:

Guest X's private jet has arrived.

We stare up, but the clouds are too low for us to see what's literally over our heads.

Will this nightmare never end?

"At least we've already vetted Xiāng," I point out. "Since you'll have your hands full with the other divorcées, bright and early tomorrow I'll vet Guest X."

Or something.

Jack's kiss is tender. "I'll get back as soon as I can… but don't wait up."

Not something a wife wants to hear.

What a gal won't do to save the world.

13

Default

A debtor's failure to make timely payments of interest and principal as they become due or to meet some other provision of a bond indenture is known as a default.

In other words, no matter how much you wish to avoid it, there comes a time in which you must "pay the Piper," as it were. And with interest.

Or end up fired, disgraced, with your credit ruined, or even worse, in jail.

Do yourself a favor: avoid this at all costs.

Even if it means doing without.

Because—bottom line—the only thing that counts is self-respect.

And you can't have that without the appreciation of others.

I wake up alone.

Was Gang with Sabine or Yulia? Last night, both

women's cabanas were dark when I passed them on the way to mine, so I have no idea.

Is Jack now with Gang's conquest?

Seeing that this is the conference's opening day, the last thing he should have done is pull an all-nighter. Otherwise, he'll drag through the assignment the rest of the day.

Since I know the cabana assigned to Guest X and I still have a cart with a few bottles of wine, several storm lamps, and enough towels to start a middle-of-nowhere tropical island no-tel motel, I don't need to bother Emmanuel. I'm sure he's got his hands full as it is, what with the storm and the never-ending demands of all the well-monied new arrivals.

At least, those who are still alive.

When Jack resurfaces, we'll give Emmanuel the bad news about the five bankers whose exterminations have created several vacancies. He won't be happy about it. But, hey, it's the cost of doing business with terrorists and rapists.

Not to mention spies out to stop the bad guys.

Okay, maybe four deaths weren't mission-related, but they were justified.

I must pass Sabine's first to get to Guest X's cabana. Her passionate groans are loud enough that I shudder. At the same time, they are like the silent dog whistle that lures any hungry mutts within range. I'm too curious about Jack's progress to stop myself from sneaking onto the veranda and peeking through Sabine's window.

She's on top, humping, bucking, and rutting. Her

lover's ecstatic groan is all I need to hear to know why, now eight hours later, Jack is still with Sabine.

Seriously? What the hell?

Now they're giggling. A moment later, she shrieks, "Yet again? *Mon ami*, you are truly living up to your motto: 'Service delivered with a smile!'"

I've heard enough.

When this mission is over, I'll have to face the fact my marriage is too.

Two guards stand in front of the cabana assigned to Guest X. When they see me, one walks over. His jacket opens slightly when he shifts, revealing a weapon strapped to his hip.

At that moment, the cabana's door opens. My eyes are drawn to the man who steps out:

Aunt Phyllis's husband, Porter Crosby, is Lee's senior agent in his Secret Service detail.

Seeing me, Porter's eyes go wide. Then he laughs—at my expense since he knows I'm supposedly on vacation.

He waves me over. "Talk about a small world!"

"You're telling me!" After kissing his cheek, I add, "Apparently not small enough. I hope you left the rest of the family in good health."

"Happy and hearty. However, Phyllis has her hands full with Trisha and her sidekick, Janie. Their new life mission is keeping Jeff smitten with her." He rolls his eyes. "For once, I think Lee regrets that Lion Lair is so close to the Stone-Craig menagerie."

I chuckle. "I'm glad he's got a sense of humor about it."

"How about Jack?" Porter asks.

I snicker. "The last topic I want to bring up with Jack is the emotional longings of any Chiffray."

This has Porter laughing loud enough to bring someone else to the cabana's door:

Lee.

Seeing me, his smile broadens. "Mrs. Craig! Fancy meeting you here."

"Believe it or not, I was just in the neighborhood—that is, Jack and I are here at the resort on what was supposed to be a vacation."

"What changed?" he asks.

"Perhaps we should go inside," I suggest.

Lee's smile disappears as he waves me in.

He points to the suite's half-moon rattan sectional. It faces the cabana's lagoon and the mountain peak on its far side. The view is so stunningly beautiful that I have to shift my eyes away to focus on the task at hand: describing what danger Lee and the rest of the conference attendees are facing.

Papers are strewn over the coffee table. A bottle of wine is already opened. As he beckons me to sit down, he notices the bottle in my hand. "Should we open yours instead?"

"Hardly! It's drugged."

Lee's double-take is priceless.

"I'll have whatever you're having." I nod at the half-filled glass on the coffee table, also a red wine.

Lee goes to the sidebar and grabs another glass. Then, after filling it, he hands it to me.

I hold it up to him. "Here's to weathering two dangerous events at once."

Lee taps it with his.

We drink. I savor its rich berry facets before launching into my tale of woe: "Yesterday, Jack and I found a dead body in our lagoon: a woman's, naked and anchored to a yacht called the Zero-Sum Game. She was our concierge: Tisa, a local. Her brother, Emmanuel, also works here, managing the resort. We were questioned by Tasmanian law enforcement while it conducted background checks on us. Upon learning our professions as intelligence assets to the United States, we were told that a terrorist attack was to take place during the financial summit and were asked to be its eyes, ears, and first line of defense."

"Then they've left the rest of us in great hands."

'That's kind of you to say."

"I'm not flattering you. It's the simple truth. With as many scrapes as you've saved me from, I know this better than anyone."

"Well, thank you. It's been a privilege." Now I'm blushing. "DNI Branham briefed us on the severity of the issue. The bottom line is that, as of yet, the US doesn't know who is behind the attack, let alone who will initiate it. We'll have to eliminate suspects from those in attendance or those serving them. We also have to vet and monitor guests on the island."

"How many suspects aren't registered attendees or event staff?"

"Of the hotel staff, there are thirty; more than one for every cabana. However, Emmanuel, the hotel manager, can vouch for them. He insists that each went through an extensive international background check."

"As for the guests?"

"There are twenty attending bankers, two conference planners, three wealthy divorcées, and the attorney finalizing their settlements."

"You forgot the partridge in a pear tree." Lee's smile fades. "Let me guess. Jack is vetting the female targets."

I roll my eyes. "Yep. As we speak, Jack is undercover—and all that implies. Thus far, we've found no evidence of an attack. At least none that implicates the attendees or staff."

When Lee's look turns to pity, I look away, feigning interest in the cabana's spectacular view.

It isn't an act. For a mere moment, I allow myself to take it in.

"Just beautiful," I murmur.

"Yes."

I glance over. Lee is looking at me. Meeting my gaze, he turns away. "Eve wasn't tempted to join you?" I ask.

Must I remind him that he's now engaged?

To my dismay, his grimace makes it obvious I must.

"She would have, but with Harrison starting preschool and Janie starting middle school—not to mention the wedding planning..." He sighs.

"Trouble in Paradise?"

"Paradise is here," he reminds me. "Back home is the real world." Lee shrugs. "Let's just say Mason left her with enough doubts that she seems to be getting cold feet."

Mason Ledbetter, a chess master who was the draw at another of Lee's projects—a worldwide youth chess competition—turned out to be a Russian asset. I found that out the hard way when he kidnapped me to sell me to the highest bidder among our enemies of state.

"In any regard, Eve felt it was best to stay home. And besides, this trip was supposed to be a quick one. The incoming storm seems to have changed that." Lee shakes his head. "As the keynote speaker, I will discuss how my foundation works with international banks by introducing and funding innovative technologies in developing coun-tries." He pours a second glass for us both. "Afterward, you and Jack are welcome to ride back with me."

"Thanks for the offer. We'll know when you take the podium if it's a false alert. If so, we may take you up on your offer." I shrug. "Or I may, anyway—if Jack hasn't resurfaced."

Lee moves closer—enough to see the tears glazing my eyes.

"Donna, seriously: doesn't Jack's—and your—honey-trap roles wear thin?"

"We've learned to put it in perspective. You know that."

Lee shakes his head. "I beg to differ. You've come to accept it. And he's come to expect you to live with the choice… with one exception."

I know what he's thinking:

Except when it comes to Lee.

"Jack now realizes you love Eve—that you're *in love* with Eve." And why Lee asked Jack to be his best man.

"Yes, I love Eve." He looks away.

"That's not what I said. It should be easy to say you're *in love* with Eve."

Lee's sigh is long. "It's hard to break old habits."

"Lee, I'm not a 'habit.' I'm a friend. But I can only stay that way if you're willing to accept it's nothing more than that. You can't make it into something that it's not. Otherwise, this fantasy of yours will hurt too many others: me, Jack, Eve—and you too—"

And that's when he kisses me.

I can't lie to myself. It's…

Not bad.

Great, in fact.

As soul-affirming as I'd always wondered.

But I'm not his soul mate.

So, I pull away—

Only to find Porter standing in the doorway.

Oh…

Shite.

At least he looks concerned, not disgusted.

Will he tell Aunt Phyllis? Even if they weren't married—even if he weren't my dear friend—I'd feel as ashamed if he had the wrong idea of this situation.

Quickly, Porter turns around. The next thing I hear him say is, "Yes, Jack, she just arrived and is bringing the boss man up to date on the situation. They're both anxious to learn your take on it."

Lee eases away. Still, he stays at my side.

Do I look guilty? To ensure the answer is no, I think about what Jack has probably been doing this past hour. Then I remember my immediate reaction to Lee's reckless and impulsive act: sadness at his unwillingness to accept my friendship without his longing for it to be more.

In one regard, Lee is spot on: Jack has no right to be jealous of my relationship with Lee just because he can so quickly turn off his emotions to fuck others when our mission calls for it —something I avoid at all costs. It doesn't matter that the targets are ready, willing, and able or that he has no emotional attachment to them. Neither do I, to mine. And, like him, I only feel derision. Sex is just a means to an end.

The difference is the perception that the conquest is his, not the unsuspecting mark.

Jack is the victor.

But when I play the sparrow, my targets aren't there to fall in love with me; I'm just a conquest, another notch on their belt.

A victim.

At least, that's how they view it.

Lucky me.

Lucky him.

All the more reason Jack's jealousy over Lee's feelings for me is bullshit.

He has no right to play the victim.

"Don't you two look cozy." Even as Jack pats Lee

on the back, he cocks a brow to show his not-so-subtle disapproval at our too-close proximity.

To demonstrate how little his jealous barb means to me, I giggle. "If you think this looks snug, you should have seen us a moment ago. Lee knows how to show a lady why he'll always be 'the one who got away.'"

Lee gawks at me as if I've lost my mind.

Jack reacts as I'd suspect: his curiosity and suspicion are masked with an icy smile. "No surprise there. "I wish I had time to be jealous. Unfortunately, we're up against a ticking clock."

"Are you divulging the pillow talk between you and one of your new friends?" I ask.

"Yes." Jack's tone couldn't be any blunter. "I'm sure that, like me, you'll feel it was worth the effort. We now know that at least one of the divorcées is a suspect."

"Which one?" I ask.

"I can't say for sure," he admits. "But she's not working alone."

"Considering you're practically strangers, your new friend was quite chatty," I point out. "Are you sure she wasn't feeding you a line?"

"Her celebrity status is her cover," Jack explains. "In truth, she's an asset for an ally."

"Which one?" I ask.

"France. She's an operative with TRACFIN, the French intelligence agency investigating money laundering and tracking down those who finance terrorism."

Well, surprise, surprise. At least we now know that Sabine is on our side.

Still, I'm wary. "If so, why did she blurt that out to you, a perfect stranger?"

Jack's face turns beet red. "We aren't 'perfect strangers.' Our paths crossed on a previous occasion: when I lived in Paris."

"You knew her before you met me?"

"Yes." He shrugs.

"And…"

"And what?"

"How well did you know her?"

"Well enough to know she's a white hat." He sighs.

Is it because he's miffed that I don't believe he's innocent, or because he's buying time?

"If you remember, even back then, my cover as Acme's VP of New Ventures meant hobnobbing with suspects—including the rich and famous," he explains. "When I was based in Paris, we met at some fancy soirée thrown by her at-the-time fiancé's investment firm. Acme had reason to believe he was laundering money for the Russians. I thought she was drunk enough to let loose with a few choice tidbits on some of his contacts that Acme had already identified as embedded cells. When I dropped their names, she grew suspicious of me. I didn't realize the necklace she wore was a facial recognition device. When her ComInt team uploaded my photo into InterPol's facial recognition system, my name popped up as an Acme operative. Her team immediately contacted Ryan to verify her true identity. We went our merry ways, but our mission teams kept each other informed of each other's progress."

I'm silent. No way in hell will I give him the satisfaction that his supposedly innocent answer got under my skin—let alone that he's off the hook for last night's disappearing act. Finally, I retort: "He's the man with whom she's now negotiating a settlement?"

"Hardly! Though the M.O. is the same. He's just as wealthy, and he's a philanderer." Jack glares at Lee. "He's like a lot of men—you know, the ones who think their wealth and power gives them a pass on fidelity to their wives—*or their fiancées.*"

The way Lee is bristling, I better change the subject—and quickly. "I'm sure Rufus will get her a great settlement."

"Either way, when she leaves here, she'll return to TRACFIN. She's always had the perfect cover for an operative: Eurotrash. By that, I mean she has looks, money, and is a renowned party animal."

"She's Eurotrash, alright," I huff. "And now she's two divorcées down and one to go."

"Not to mention Rufus, their lawyer," Jack points out.

"Your divorcée chum doesn't have a read on him yet?"

"His background checks out, but something about him bothers her. She just can't put her finger on it." Jack smirks. "But I'm sure you'll figure it out—if you can tear yourself away from Lee long enough to take it on."

"You both have your hands full, so feel free to go your merry way," Lee declares. "Donna, the offer for a lift home after the event still stands." Without turning, he adds, "You too, Jack."

"Gee, thanks," Jack's tone drips with sarcasm. "Then

again, since it gives you more face time with my wife, maybe not." Jack reaches up to Lee's face—

And wipes my signature gloss off Lee's lips.

Taken aback, Lee shoves him away. Instinctively, Jack lunges at Lee—

Only to be tackled by two of Lee's Secret Service agents. They pin him to the floor until Porter says, "Jack, perhaps now is not the best time or place for this conversation."

"Thanks to your boss's goon squad, I guess that day will never come." His retort is muffled since his face is against the floor's jute rug.

"I think we've worn out our welcome." My tone is so cheery that Jack guffaws. At least he's no longer struggling.

Still, Lee's men wait for Jack's nod before lifting him onto his feet.

Lee gives my hand a goodbye squeeze.

I'm relieved he leaves it at that. I'd find it difficult to explain to the kids how their dad ended up in prison for life.

14

Trust

*T*rust *is the term for a legal entity granted separate and distinct rights, similar to a person or corporation. In a trust, a party known as a trustee has been given the right to hold title, manage, and distribute assets of another party known as the trustor for the benefit of a third party, the beneficiary, as per the trustor's wishes. This arrangement reduces paperwork and estate taxes.*

In relationship terms, it's a triangle in which one party gives, another receives, and the person in the middle does all the heavy lifting.

As with most three ways, invariably, someone walks away dissatisfied.

In blunt terms, they feel as if they got screwed.

They'd probably be right.

We're halfway back to our cabana when finally Jack speaks: "Why did you go to Lee?"

I stop so suddenly that he bumps into me. "Seriously, Jack? In the first place, I didn't 'go to Lee. Per our mission, I delivered towels, a gift box, and wine to Guest X. Someone had to do it. Did you expect me to sit around and twiddle my thumbs until you resurfaced?"

Jack looks up at the sky as if he'll find what he means to say somewhere in the storm clouds roiling above us. Then, glaring, he barks, "Let me rephrase the question. Up until now, we've tag-teamed on that endeavor. Why didn't you wait for me to go with you?"

"You broke that protocol last night when you insisted I *not* accompany you to vet the other divorcées. Have you forgotten that?" I snarl. "Twelve hours later, I felt it was now or never, with or without you, to make our usual delivery to Guest X's cabana—*whose identity had not yet been revealed to me.* When it was, you better believe I felt Lee deserved to know what was going on! You don't think it was wise?"

Silently, Jack glowers.

"Oh, and by the way: I walked by your target's cabana to make sure you haven't been murdered and buried in some dark hole, only to discover you were *still in the whore's bed!* "

"I—I fell asleep. I was dead tired, and it… *it just… happened.*"

"Something was happening alright," I mutter.

"Speak for yourself," Jack retorts. "Had I walked in just a few seconds later—and without an armed escort— who knows how far you'd have let Lee go!"

"*As if!* Don't try to project your guilt onto me. You and your delicious divorcée were going at it with gusto!

Tell me something. If you already knew her cover, why go through the gymnastics routine?"

He's speechless. But it doesn't last long. Throwing up his arms, he lets loose with a derisive guffaw. "You're either nuts or creating some fantasy to justify what I interrupted in there." Jack goes nose to nose with me. "Be honest, Donna: did you mention your frustration with my role in the mission?"

He sees his answer in my blush.

Defensively, I retort, "He's my friend. He asked. I answered."

"In other words, Lee played on your insecurities in the hope you'd cry on his shoulder—and then be receptive to his conniving excuse to kiss you."

"Which is less than you did with that…that woman!"

"As I emphatically told you, *I didn't do anything with her.*"

"Liar! And now you'll move on to the next lovely lady…and the next—"

"It's what we do—remember?"

"All too well. I'm never allowed to forget it!" I'm so loud that even the incoming squall can't mute my shout.

Damn it.

"Well, at least we can borrow munitions and a satellite phone from Lee's security detail," I say.

"Secret Service protocol would forbid them releasing any weaponry to us," he counters.

"If Lee insisted, they concede," I point out. "You can't let your pride get in the way, Look, if you can't keep your cool until he can explain what exactly we're to do, and to whom, maybe I should talk to him alone."

"Oh, no, you don't! Wouldn't he love that—knowing that he figured out a way to ruin our vacation *and* that he can talk to you without censuring himself because I won't be listening in."

"Is it my fault he's infatuated with me?"

"Yes—*because you lead him on!*"

"Pray tell, why are you accusing me of doing that?"

"Because I saw it with my own eyes," Jack retorts. "You kissed Lee! Or have you conveniently forgotten that? Oh, and by the way, *your gloss on his lips didn't help your case.*"

"You've got it backward. He kissed me."

Jack growls, "*I knew it!* He can't leave you alone!" He stalks away, only to come back. Glaring, he asks, "Tell the truth: did you like it?"

My silence speaks volumes.

"Ah… So, that's how it is."

"Have you forgotten he's now a happily engaged man?" The lie sticks in my throat.

"Yeah, sure…*whatever.*" Jack rolls his eyes.

"What does that mean: 'whatever?'"

"It means you'll always be the one that got away." Jack throws up his hands. "Sure then, go ahead and beg. Lee would love that. You probably wouldn't have to get down on your hands and knees." He smirks. "But if you did, he'd eat it up with a spoon. And you could—"

I slap his face so hard that he loses his footing.

"You disgust me." My voice trembles so much that I can barely get the words out.

Jack walks ahead.

And he expects me to follow him.

I do because I have nowhere else to go.

Jack does. It takes him three minutes to shrug on a jacket and pocket a toothbrush.

"Where are you going?"

"There's still some vetting to do. Remember?"

"Ah, yes! How could I forget that there's yet another divorcée who hasn't been quote-unquote vetted?"

Jack storms out.

I watch as he takes the path toward the lagoon where the women reside.

He didn't even take a change of underwear. Then again, he wouldn't be in it long, so why bother?

Nothing stops me from weathering the storm with Lee in his cabana except knowing it's exactly what Jack assumes I'll do.

Instead, I head over to the concierge cabana. I must confess to Emmanuel about the five bankers who won't attend the conference and why.

15

White Collar Crime

For your typical housewife, the term "white-collar crime" can have one of two meanings. The first one her brain gravitates toward with disgust is the thought that (Quelle horreur!) she let Hubby out of the house with a ring around the collar.

But another walk of shame is much worse. It would be his, with hands cuffed, if it were discovered he'd absconded with his clients' hard-earned savings.

After the trial, the sentencing, the conviction, and his incarceration, you'd be allowed periodic conjugal visits—

If you want them.

If you can guess the password of his off-shore bank account, no need to drop off freshly laundered prison-authorized shirts, and you can live the life he always dreamed for himself—

Including having someone else do your laundry.

Emmanuel's assistant politely suggests I cool my heels while he's in a staff meeting.

I've tried to clarify that I have something important to report, but nothing I say raises an eyebrow, only a mocking smirk. Now that I'm no longer a guest but one of the staff, I suppose I'm not worthy of her courtesy.

Truly rude, considering how I'm trying to save everyone's life—including hers.

I'll let Emmanuel remind her of that.

In the meantime, I wait.

And wait.

And wait.

Finally, the door to Emmanuel's office opens. About twenty men walk out. All are muscular and dressed as concierges. The tallest of them—over seven and a half feet—has deep green eyes. Seeing me, Jolly Green Giant winks, then licks his lips.

No need to encourage him. I scratch my nose with my middle finger.

For some reason, he finds this funny. Go figure.

None smile. Emmanuel must have told them what we're up against and has asked them to be on high alert.

Seeing me, he nods his request that I follow him into his office.

As I do, he closes the door behind us.

"Has your vetting been successful?" he asks.

I want to share some good news: "Thus far, we've discovered no munitions. This leads us to believe that no attendees are involved in sabotage."

The relief shows itself in his sigh. "Perhaps the authorities have it wrong, and this event isn't a terrorist target after all," he suggests. "If you take your leave now, I would vouch that you did what was asked of you."

"Thank you, Emmanuel. But with the storm sitting right on top of us, I don't think anyone is going anywhere." Now for the bad news: "I do have a few items of importance to report: the deaths of five bankers."

Emmanuel's jaw drops open. "Who? And how?"

"Three occurred during a poker game. It involved the Americans: Howard Krebs, Edward Randall Morton the Third, and Phillip Wallburton. Let's say that…well, things got out of hand. They attacked—"

"*Each other*? Such lunacy! Knowing the finances these men deal with, the stakes are high. And yes, the ruckus happened *over a game…*" He shakes his head in wonder. "Well, that is truly unimaginable!"

I stay silent. What possible advantage would there be in admitting they attempted to rape me—and perhaps film my death as a snuff film—but that I fought back hard enough that they were killed instead?

No, it's best to keep that to myself.

"As I mentioned, there were also two other deaths."

Emmanuel sighs. "Whose?"

"One was Blaine Wentworth, the Canadian banker. He committed suicide: a gunshot to the head. He also admitted to having been part of the terrorism plot."

Astounded, Emmanuel leaps up. "He said that to you?"

"Yes. He was disillusioned and ashamed of himself."

Anxious, Emmanuel paces the floor. Finally, he stops to look out the window. Rain pelts its panes with the fierceness of a heavy metal drummer. "Did he name his accomplices?"

"Sadly, no. However, there are at least three suspects: a Slavic woman, an American male, and a British male. Maybe just two, if Blaine was mistaken for the American, or if one of the three American bankers' involvement somehow escaped our scrutiny."

Emmanuel sighs, relieved. "Which lends even more credence to the premise that the authorities may have faulty intelligence. With that in mind, what is your next move?"

"The conference begins in an hour. All we can do is be on our guard," I admit. "To that end, I recommend that Jack and I attend in the guise we've held for the past day—that is, as concierge staff."

Emmanuel nods. "Since you've elected to stay until the storm ends, I welcome your participation."

"Thank you, I reply. "About the men who just left here: I assume they and the other staff members have been apprised of the dire situation and will also be on guard?"

"That is correct. Sadly, since the only known suspect has killed himself, all we can do now is keep our eyes open for his accomplices. Like you, my staff needs to know who they can trust. You and Jack should feel free to introduce yourself to them before the keynote speech."

"We will indeed. By the way, the conference's keynote speaker—former President Lee Chiffray—is a dear friend."

"Ah, good to know!" Emmanuel pauses. "Please feel free to make his safekeeping your priority."

"I'd like it to be Jack's mission," I insist. I only say this because I know Jack will hate it.

Well, too bad.

"If you feel that is best, then so be it," Emmanuel replies. He hands me four notes. "By the way, I'd like you to deliver this to our other guests—the women here for their divorces and Monsieur Coulter. Gretta would like them to join us for the dinner and the keynote. I'm sure they'll be enthralled with Mr. Chiffray."

I can't argue with him on that. And, if so, it should drive Jack up a wall.

Since he's positioned as merely the help, I'll enjoy watching his conquests throw him over for a power ranger of Lee's caliber.

"Donna, one last thing." Emmanuel stands up, goes to a bookcase, and picks up one of the guest boxes. Like those given to the divorcées, it's pink. "Before all this excitement, you were a guest—and a treasured one. But you were never given one of these."

I chuckle. "Considering what is inside, I'll say thanks, but no thanks."

His face falls. "What do you mean?"

"Frankly, the last thing I need is a pair of pink handcuffs." There's no need to tell him that Jack and I aren't exactly on playful terms right now.

Suddenly, Emmanuel laughs. I see why when he opens the box. There are no cuffs. However, the box holds two silver digital pads. "Open one of the pads," he insists.

I do as he asks. Photos float onto the screen. One was taken the day we arrived. Others have beautiful views from the island's various peaks and lagoons. Recipes also appear, highlighting some of the delicious meals we enjoyed and the drinks we were served.

"I'd prefer that you always remember Kisiwa Cha Paradiso and me, at our best—before things became dire."

"Thank you, Emmanuel. I'd prefer that too." I take it from him. Now that we've exhausted all talk of business, it's time I break the hard news: "A final topic: one of the dead bankers was Tisa's murderer."

Shocked, Emmanuel steadies himself by sitting down. "How did you learn this?"

"The banker—the Swiss national, Oskar Surbeck— kept the bracelet you gave Tisa." I hand it to him.

Emmanuel stares down at it. Finally, he picks it up and slips it into his jacket pocket. "I know how much she loved it. I greatly appreciate your having retrieved it for me."

"She was a kind, loving person. I'm sorry for your loss."

He doesn't respond. Instead, he looks down at his desk.

Silently, I take my leave.

I'm already outside the cabana when I realize I have no umbrella.

I don't want to go back for it. Emmanuel needs his privacy.

By the time I get back to our cabana, I'm soaked.

I head for the shower, only to find Jack is in it. Seeing me, he turns off the water and grabs a towel. He doesn't look me in the eye when he asks: "Where were you?"

"Where do you think I was?" I retort. Of course, I already know what he thinks:

That I was with Lee.

If he's so insecure that he wants to think the worst, far be it from me to beg him to do otherwise.

He stands still as if calculating what to say next. Will he settle for yet another accusation? Or will he humble-brag about his conquests and then go back to his usual whine: that being an undercover lover is a tough job, but someone has to do it?

If instead he chooses to harp about Lee's infatuation with me—well, frankly—

I don't want to play this game anymore.

Ha! I've just thought of a way to nip it in the bud, once and for all: "Despite the storm and the power outage, Emmanuel is prepared for the attendees to congregate in the Summit Cabana in less than an hour. You have a special assignment. You're to be the liaison with Lee's security detail."

He scowls. "Like hell I will!"

"It's at Emmanuel's request. If you have an issue with that, speak to him yourself."

"Sure, I'll do it now. I'll tell him what I will say to your boyfriend—and, for that matter, you too: from now on, I'm a free agent."

Free agent? Is that what he wants to call the breakup of our marriage?

I'm too shocked to hold back my tears.

But not my fist. I punch him in his gut.

As he doubles over, I hiss, "Not to worry, Jack. If that's what you want, I'll start divorce proceedings. Since it's even quicker to do it here, I'll file right now. But in the meantime, if you can stay away from your tantalizing whore du jour, try not to get us killed on this tropical hellscape. That's my game plan, anyway. But if I leave it as a widow, so be it."

"First Babette, now you! One thing you can say about Lee: he has a type." Jack smirks in mock amazement. "I'm sure he'll be delighted to let yet another merry widow cry on his shoulder—let alone be swept down the aisle by him."

This earns Jack a sidekick that sends him toppling backward.

I walk out, though I have nowhere to go.

And then I remember the one person who would be happy to see me: Rufus Coulter.

He's getting his wish: a *Hot Housewife of Hilldale* is hiring him for her divorce.

This time, I take Jack's umbrella.

16

Joint and Several Liability

This is a legal term for a responsibility shared by two or more parties to a lawsuit.

In other words, if you are the wronged party, sue all the bastards!

You can also collect the total damages awarded by a court from any or all of them since, in such cases, responsibility for the total amount awarded would be shared by all.

And don't worry if one of the parties fails to pay; the others' obligation to pay will increase.

That way, you'll get something out of this bad experience for everyone involved.

~

"Well, ain't you a sight for sore eyes!" Rufus sits on a barstool in front of the resort's outside tiki bar. He seems to be nursing a Bloody Mary and a hangover.

"Late night?"

His nod comes with a gravelly croak. "Ninety percent of my job is babysitting. Usually, the weather, the ambiance, and a steady supply of frozen margaritas make this gig a well-paid cakewalk. But between this damn storm and just one piece of man candy for the ladies to share—and that's if I stick to my supply of Little Blue Pills—you could say I've been ridden hard and put away wet." He rolls his eyes. "To my great relief, they've found a new playpal." He nods in the direction of Sabine's cabana. "From what I can tell, that husband of yours has the sort of staying power that would make him an asset to my business. If he had a law degree, I'd even consider making him an associate."

"You mean a partner, don't you?"

Rufus snorts. "You drive a hard bargain, little lady."

"Not to worry. I'm neither his pimp nor his head-hunter." I blink away my tears. "Consider yourself my attorney for my imminent divorce."

Rufus's face falls flatter than a soufflé. "Aw, hell! If you two lovebirds can't make it, who can?"

"Twenty-four hours ago, I would have felt the same way." I force a smile onto my lips. "One of your clients made an end-run—or maybe I should call it a front-run—that knocked me out of the running."

He drops his head and sighs. "Full disclosure: this gig broke up my marriage. I'm sorry to see it do the same to yours."

"Thanks for your honesty." Gently, I kiss his cheek.

"*Shee*-it! After that, you better believe I'd be ashamed to hire him!"

My laugh comes out as a snort. "I'm sure you'd get

over it." I hand Rufus the four invitations from Emmanuel. "You and your clients are invited to the dinner, which will take place in about an hour. The keynote speaker is former U.S. President Lee Chiffray."

Hearing that, Rufus sits up straight. "You don't say! Well, I'm sure my stable of fillies will want to hear what he's got to say!" He winks at me. "Especially since he's single."

"He is at that," I admit. "But not for long. He's got a fiancée." I say it like I mean it. I do because I genuinely believe Lee isn't stupid enough to ditch Eve.

Especially not for me.

Even Jack's boneheadedness isn't enough to make me reconsider my alternatives. Two husbands in one lifetime is enough for me.

Speaking of which, I can't help but ask: "Whose bed did Jack end up in last night?"

Rufus rolls his eyes. "A better question is, who didn't he sleep with?"

I already have that answer: me. "I'm not asking who Jack screwed but who he spent the night with."

"Ah—gotcha!" Rufus thinks for a moment. "From what I remember, it was the insatiable Sabine."

"Not Yulia?"

"Nah. That turned out to be a one-and-done." Rufus shrugs.

"On her end, or his?"

"If you're asking if she kicked him out of her bed, I can only say that, at the most, they were together for a half-hour, tops." He raises a brow. "They may have eaten supper before they said Grace, but it took less time than a Happy Meal."

Ouch! So, our prime suspect kicked Jack out of her bed! That must have bruised his ego.

As opposed to Jack's fucking—what he does with targets—his lovemaking (what he only did with me until now) is slow and steady but then crescendos to an immensely satisfying orgiastic symphony.

Yep, Jack sure knows how to swing his baton.

In any event, if what Rufus says is true, Yulia is less than impressed.

"Admittedly, that's not up to Jack's usual standards," I concede.

Rufus leans in and divulges, "If you ask me, I think she's still pining for the dude who tossed her over."

"The French capitalist?"

"They weren't married, but he signed a palimony agreement before she moved in permanently. Three years of his philandering was all she could take before she rang me up." He tips his glass at me. "The rest, as they say, will soon be history." He looks at his watch. "By this time tomorrow."

"Is that your way of saying she may not want to say goodbye to her soon-to-be ex, despite all the grief he's put her through?"

"All I can tell you is that her rutting session with Jack was shorter and less rambunctiously vocal than his and Sabine's, whose dirty talk is operatic—both in its drama and its decibel count!" The thought awes him enough to merit a head shake. "Of course, Sabine is naturally horizontal, if you catch my drift." Noting my scowl, he quickly adds, "Hey, I get it: *sore subject.*" Rufus's voice trails off—no need to point out the obvious.

Time to change the topic. "Listen, Jack should be coming this way soon. Remind him that Emmanuel wants him to liaise with Chiffray's security team."

Rufus looks at his watch. "Will do. I should go round up the ladies since this shindig starts any moment now. I should rouse Xiãng first since she's a heavy sleeper."

"That's a very charitable term for her addiction."

"In this job, sometimes it's best to parse words." His shoulders fall at my blunt description of her problem. "Hey, it drives me nuts. Yulia, as well. She doesn't understand why Xiãng is so self-destructive when she's got so much to live for."

"Admittedly, she's got a point." I have to ask. "What does Sabine think of it?"

Rufus frowns. "Sabine only thinks of herself. I'm sure Jack would agree with me."

"Don't remind me." My tone is warning enough that Rufus backs away—

But then something makes his bleary eyes light up. "Well, speak of the devil!"

I follow his gaze. He doesn't mean Yulia, but Xiãng and Sabine.

I look skyward. "Don't you mean 'devils'?"

Rufus guffaws. "To-*may*-toe, to-*mah*-toe." He waves them over.

Since that's the last thing I need I turn to leave—

Only to have Rufus throw his arm around my shoulder. "Come on over, ladies, and meet the latest addition to our entourage, the soon-to-be Mrs. ex-Jack Craig!"

His news certainly gets their attention. Though curious enough to stroll over to see whose plaything they stole, Sabine and Xiăng's glances are cursory at best. It's obvious to them why Jack's eye wandered their way.

Rufus hands them the invitations. "For a free brunch, ladies—and the *piece de resistance*: new man meat! The bankers' boondoggle is being regaled by our former President of the *U*-Nited States: the honorable Lee Chiffray!"

Hearing this, Sabine's eyes glitter like cut sapphires. "You will arrange an introduction, *oui*, Rufus?"

"Why, of course, darlin'! I'm here to serve." To prove it, he pats her comely rump. "And I know you'll make the photo op count." He winks knowingly.

Upon hearing this, even Xiăng perks up—

But not for long. "Damn this storm! If it weren't for the power outage, I could live-stream it to my followers!" That realization takes the wattage out of Xiăng's Blue-Steel sulk.

"Not to worry," Rufus insists. "If the electricity finally comes on, it'll happen first at the event cabana. Emmanuel is no dummy. He's got one shot to make this puddle-jump a Tropical Davos." He snaps his fingers. "Hey, I'll bet you're just the right ladies to convince him that this is also the perfect location for a presidential version of *The Bachelor*, so let's do this."

I think I'm going to throw up.

"And if he won't invest in that, no matter. You lovely ladies look just as fetching by candlelight. I'm sure the bankers will second that." He chucks Sabine's chin.

"Diex merci, tomorrow we leave this island," Sabine coos. "The weather is *mérde*!"

Rufus arches a brow. "As for the sex?"

I force myself to smile. I won't give him the satisfaction of getting my goat.

"*C'était le marveleus!*" Sabine sighs blissfully. "It will be the only thing worth remembering about this *voyage*." She follows Xiãng up the path to the event cabana.

Rufus waits until she's out of earshot before declaring, "I'll start your divorce paperwork, darling Donna. I'll even pre-date it so you can leave with the rest of us."

Oh, joy.

At least Jack wasn't with them.

So then, where is he?

Perhaps our cabana.

Is he packing up or wanting to make up?

I have to know where we stand, so I head back.

I'm halfway to the event cabana when something catches my eye: a pink digital device.

Sabine's name is monogrammed on it.

How the hell did it end up out here?

Maybe it fell out of her purse. I look around to see if other items, usually in a purse, are also strewn about, but I don't see anything.

I pocket it. When I see her, I'll hand it over.

Or maybe I'll beat her to death with it for breaking up my marriage.

I'm about to turn down the path to our cabana when I see Yulia coming my way.

What the hell was she doing in our lagoon?

17

Human Capital

The economic value of a worker, measured in skills, education, training, intellect, and experience, is known as "human capital." An investment in human capital increases productivity and, therefore, profitability.

A relationship is also an investment in human capital. You invest time in finding someone with intellect, humor, a pleasing personality, good health, and great looks. Making the first four attributes a priority will ensure a successful relationship. The last trait is just icing on the cake!

～

When Yulia sees me, she attempts a smile. But I'm sure my scowl is the reason she finally gives up. Still, she falls into lockstep. "I gather you are Jack's wife?"

Despite her excellent English, her Slavic accent pronounces my husband's name with an A long enough to sound as if she said *Jacques*.

I don't—and *I won't*—give her the satisfaction of acknowledging her interest in me. Instead, I look straight ahead when I retort, "Yeah. For the time being, anyway."

My response causes Yulia's eyes to widen, if only momentarily. When our stares meet, she looks away.

It's too much to assume her distress is from compassion—more like pity.

Shrugging, she gets to the point: "He mentioned you are close to the former president. I want a private moment with Monsieur Chiffray. If you could make the introduction immediately when we arrive—"

"Ain't happening."

You'd think my snarl, short and to the point, should have warned her off; hearing my emphatic response to Jack's lies about Lee and me would cause her to step back —perhaps even run in the opposite direction, right?

"Jack predicted you would respond jealously. But let me assure you, I have no intention of intruding on your, er… "

Talk about doubling down in the worst possible way! And yet, she's shut that blathering pie hole she calls a mouth for all the wrong reasons: not because the look on my face warns her that any further insults will force me to snatch the breath from her lungs like a Dementor, but because she's searching for the right word:

"…your *intimacy* with your dear friend, who—"

Worst. Choice. EVER.

"*Excuse me?* I don't know what malarkey you've been told by your—from at least, what I've heard—less than satisfying love tussles with your latest bed buddy—*who's also my philandering soon-to-be ex-husband*—so let me set the record straight once and for all about my relationship with Mr. Chiffray: Lee and I aren't—and have never been—intimate! We're just good friends, plain and simple. Got it? So, bottom line: *I can't help you.*"

I stalk off.

She follows.

I stop short.

She runs into me.

When I turn around, it's to give her a gut punch—

Which she dodges. Instead, she kicks me in the side—

And I go head-long into a thatch of ferns.

As I rise, I jerk some thick, supple vines out of the ground by their roots. In no time I've wrapped the ends around both hands, leaving a yard's length of vine between them—

This is enough to toss over Yulia's head, twist, and listen to her gag. As her hands claw at the vines, she rises—

And just as quickly slams backward into me, raising me off the ground. She ducks so fast that I somersault over her—

And land on my back so hard that the wind is knocked out of me.

As she runs off, I force myself to get up—

Along with a coconut—

Which I hurl at her.

It hits Yulia's head, knocking her out.

I'm hog-tying her when I hear: "Donna! What the hell are you doing?"

I look up at Porter. He's not alone. There's another Secret Service agent with him.

What can I tell him, that she screwed Jack, and now she has her sights on Lee? The last thing I need is to sound irrational or ashamed.

Or worst of all, jealous.

And yet, I have to say something.

He'll accept only one answer: *"She's our prime suspect."*

It's all Porter needs to hear. He nods to the other agent. "Take her to the staging barn." Nodding, the man swings her over his shoulder and hikes off.

"Where's the staging barn?" I ask.

"It's that large wooden shed outside the event cabana."

"Why there?"

"It's where one of our guys rigged up a short-wave radio transmitter. He hacked the cabana's security cameras, too. That way, we have eyes and ears on Eagle during this shindig."

"Have you also been able to contact the outside world?" I ask.

"We've put out several May Days, but so far, no response," Porter admits.

We follow the other agent and his baggage.

Or I should say, mine.

Gretta stands outside the event cabana, greeting the attendees. When she glances over, she seems surprised to see me with Porter.

As he waves her over, he warns me, "Gretta is good peeps, okay? So, come clean with her."

"Sure," I reply.

This earns me a hug.

Noting Gretta's surprise, he declares, "Ms. Ullman, Donna Craig is one of us. She's been working undercover."

Her relief shows itself with a smile and a sigh. She lays her hand on my arm. "Thank you for your help. Emmanuel never told me your true role."

"It was the best way to clear your event's participants before today," I explain. "Unfortunately, there were some casualties."

"Yes, so Mr. Crosby has mentioned." She bows her head. "I'm sorry that you were put in such a tenuous position. From what I understand, because of the communications blackout, the mainland authorities have yet to be told about the many people who have already died on this island over the past twenty-four hours. All this, and the terrorists have yet to attack!" She wipes away a tear. "If you'll excuse me now, I've got to supervise the check-in of our other guests." She hurries into the event cabana.

I head that way, too, only to find Porter on my heels. "But... You aren't on the list to work the event."

"Sure I am. Where else would I be?"

When Porter is anxious, he has a tell: he rubs his chin. Whatever he's holding back, he's keeping mum, and I don't have time for it.

I'm just about to walk in when I catch sight of Jack, Lee, and four others in his security detail heading toward us from another trail. They are dressed casually, like the other event-goers. Spotting me, Jack frowns and makes his way over.

Taking my arm, he hisses, "What are you doing here?"

I shrug off his grasp. "It's my job to be here, you idiot."

"You're supposed to be…*elsewhere!*"

"Says who?" I taunt.

Jack is about to say something, but Lee and the rest of his entourage are beside us by now.

"What's wrong?" Lee asks.

Jack glares at him. "I told you—*she cannot go in there!*"

Lee stares at Jack. "You're following through with it, then, I take it?"

"Following through with what?" I ask.

Lee shrugs but says. "Donna, in this particular instance, Jack is right. You're to stay out here." Seeing Porter's concern, Lee adds, "I mean it."

"What the—"

Before I know it, Porter has cuffed me and dragged me off, too.

Three of Lee's security detail stand at the staging shed's door. They may look casual, but they're on full alert.

Yulia, still knocked out, is now cuffed at her feet and her wrists; she lays on her side on the floor.

Too bad Jack's not here to see it.

"Does this one get ankle cuffs too?" One agent asks.

Noting the panic in my eyes, Porter shakes his head. "No. She'll behave." He turns to me. "You'll allow Yulia to make it off the island alive."

My cackle sounds hollow even to my ears. "I'll do my best. Scout's honor."

Porter waits for the official hand signal.

I sigh but then give it.

Satisfied, he hustles out the door.

Does it matter that I was never a Scout? Nah. What he doesn't know won't hurt him.

I watch the monitors. The cameras follow Jack and Lee's team entering the event cabana. They take seats at different tables but at those closest to the large raised podium, which is circular and about twenty feet in diameter.

Finally, the meal is served. Within half an hour, Lee takes the podium. He is six or seven minutes into his spiel about the enormous disparity between the world's wealthy and poor when the room suddenly darkens.

At first, everyone is too shocked to talk, let alone scream—

Until one blood-curdling cry is heard.

A single spotlight roams through the room.

Lee is gone—

And so is the rest of his team, including Jack.

The spotlight stops on one face: that of one of China's bank representatives: Hu Gang.

He is on his knees. A man stands over him: I recognize him from his height. Jolly Green Giant was the tallest of the muscled concierges leaving Emmanuel's office earlier this morning.

Gang trembles as a deep mechanical voice bellows: "Those in this room have controlled the world's purse strings for too long. You've held onto the power to starve whole nations! To bring to, and keep, whole populations on their knees, never to rise to a standard of living devoid of poverty. It is time to right that wrong!" The concierge snatches Gang by the neck so that the security cameras see what happens next:

Jolly Green cuts off his head.

He then holds it up, and the electronic notebook inscribed with Gang's name is placed in front of Gang's terror-filled eyes.

A digital tone indicates the account is open.

Jolly Green then types in some commands. On the screens throughout the room, the captives see Gangs's funds drain from his account.

They also see the internal messages between the bank's tech team, watching as the institution's coffers are drained in mere seconds. Their texts, flying across the screens, are screeds of sheer panic.

Jolly Green Giant's voice continues: "All these years, your eyes have held the world hostage. Now we are doing the same to you. You will save yourselves by unlocking your banks' vaults with your eye scans. Otherwise, you shall suffer the same fate as Hu Gang."

"But—but our bank's encryptions make it impossible for us to get beyond our personal accounts!" I recognize Alain Micheaux's voice.

Jolly Green laughs raucously. "Bring me the liar so that he can prove my point!'

The sound of struggling can be heard. Two other large concierges come into view with Alain, who is arm-locked between them. His hands are cuffed behind him.

While Jolly Green takes his electronic pad, the others hold his head steady so that it can scan his eye.

Jolly Green waits until the screams and wails die before moving to the *piece de resistance,* proving yet again that he can ruin the bankers and their banks with quick keystrokes.

A tone indicates the account is open. In one quick motion, Alain's captor twists his neck.

He dies with a gasp.

I hear a strangled cry from behind me. Yulia is also staring at the screen. Though groggy, she is alert enough to cry out in anguish. *"Alain...! Au mon dieu! Non—non!"* Her Slavic accent has disappeared. Her cuffs don't stop her from leaping down from the table, but they foil her attempt to rush to the monitor. She lays on the floor, sobbing.

"You had relations with him too?" I ask.

"'*Too?*'... " She shakes her head, confused.

"You were with Jack," I remind her. "I know you were!"

"*Non!* It was only pretend—for eavesdroppers! Didn't Jack mention my role within TRACFIN to you?"

Yulia, not Sabine, was Jack's TRACFIN connection?

Stupid, stupid me...

Before I answer, Yulia exclaims, "Look! The terrorists

are taking the electronic devices that were given as gifts for attending the symposium!"

My eyes turn to the monitor. She's right.

"Take a look around, ladies and gentlemen! Yours are the faces of greed! It will be the last you see in your final moments."

The attendees' attempts to follow them are met with a spray of bullets at the ceiling.

Through the screams and melée, I hear Porter's voice through the monitor, "Donna, there are two sets of cuff keys on the hook beside the door. You and Yulia must get out of there—*now!*"

I scan the room—

Well…duh, there are the keys. Porter, the smart ass, left them on purpose.

I run over, grab the keys, and toss a pair to Yulia.

Like me, she doesn't waste time getting out of the cuffs—

Or running out the door.

I grab the backpack and follow her.

And just in time, since mere moments later, the event cabana explodes—

The staging barn does too—

And the blast sends Yulia and me flying.

18

Conflict Theory

As conceived by Karl Marx, conflict theory is based on the notion that society is in a state of perpetual conflict caused by competition for limited resources.

Another of its premises is that social order is maintained by domination and power rather than by consensus and conformity. In Marx's worldview, those having power and wealth will do whatever is necessary to keep it. He also argued that suppressing the poor and powerless is the easiest way to do this.

I, too, have a theory: Marx came up with this cockeyed notion because a shopaholic wife—in this case, Jenny von Westphalen—henpecked him.

If I'm right, consider how different our world would be if she too had had an economic theory that whole nations had rallied around…

Perhaps they'd have called it "Fashion Week."

In any regard, food for thought.

I land hard enough to be stunned, but at least I'm in a thick patch of ferns.

Yulia is just a few feet away, but she's not moving. I check to make sure she's breathing—

Thankfully, yes.

And then she groans.

I put my hand over her mouth. When her eyes flutter open, I put a finger to my lips, then whisper, "Do you remember the blast?"

Yulia nods, but she also grimaces from her agony. "My lagoon… It is close by. There is a secret cove. It is on the right, buried deep behind the rock where all the parrots roost. They are so noisy and vicious that no one dares to go near it." Her smile lasts just a moment before she's overcome by pain again. "We can hide there."

"First, I must do some reconnaissance. Can you get there on your own?"

"Yes." To prove it, she stands. The effort comes with a wince, but she's steady.

"Good. Stay hidden. Give me a half hour. If they miss me, I'll bring help."

I won't mention where that help will come from.

When Jack and Lee and his security team disappeared from the event cabana, where did they go?

They couldn't have just dissolved into thin air!

I have to be prepared for the worst: that they died in the blast.

And what about Emmanuel? If the terrorists have him, I must help him escape. Not just for his sake but for mine too. He knows the island better than anyone.

I run to his office.

Emmanuel's office building is locked. Despite this, I'm afraid to shout his name. If any terrorists are within earshot, I don't want to draw their attention. Perhaps he's hunkering down in there.

I walk around to the back of the building. The hill on which it's built slopes downward. It's steep enough that a low window reveals a basement level. The storm has shattered the window's glass. Carefully, I climb through it.

It's a small storage room. I try the knob:

Ah, heck—it's locked—

But not for long. I rummage through a utensil drawer filled with soup bowls and spoons—

And a couple of seafood picks.

All it takes is one to pop the lock.

Afterward, I twist my hair into a bun and secure it with both picks. They'll have to do as weapons until I get ahold of something bigger; and hopefully, containing a full burst of rounds.

Slowly, silently, I climb the stairwell. When I reach the top, I open the door and peek out. I hear a voice:

Emmanuel's.

"...you can't do that..." and "...all the bodies..." then "...will soon be here..." and "leave now, before..."

I can't make out all the words, but by his tone, he's upset. "I'm warning you!"

He's their only living witness...

They are going to kill him.

I can't let that happen.

Suddenly, the door opens. Two men walk out.

I duck behind the door again so that they don't see me. They walk down the hall.

Did they tie him up? Is he alone?

Quickly, silently, I peek into his office.

Emmanuel is sitting behind his desk. His eyes are closed. Is he praying?

"Emmanuel," I whisper. "Hurry, let's go while we can."

Startled, his eyes open wide. As my face registers with him, his jaw drops. "You…were in the shed!"

"I got out just in time." I beckon for him. "I'm shocked you're also alive. But we've got to get out of here now! We don't have much time."

He nods, but he grimaces, and his eyes shift slightly.

I feel the presence of someone behind me.

My elbow goes back—hard.

The man grunts and buckles.

I pull a pick from my hair and stab him in the jugular.

He goes down.

Instinctively, I turn back to Emmanuel. He's holding a gun pointed at me.

I duck—

And just in time. It hits some other guy who had snuck up behind me with a crowbar. The blast has him staggering backward before he falls.

I pick up the crowbar and run—

Just out of range of Emmanuel's next shot, which ricochets off the wall above my head.

Okay, now I get the picture. *Why the hell did it take me so long?*

There's no one to stop me from running out of the building. So that Emmanuel can't do the same, I stick one of the seafood picks into the lock so that he can't get out, at least for now—

This begs the question: Where are the rest of his thugs?

My guess: they're chasing down anyone who got away.

Since I fit that description, I'm out of here.

For once, I thank god for this belligerent storm.

Its ceaseless howls drown out the crackles of limbs and leaves as I run toward the path that takes me to Yulia's lagoon.

Sheets of rain obscure me from the men who pass within yards of me, cursing the sting of the bullet-hard pelting drizzle blown at them sideways.

Thankfully, Yulia is right where she said she'd be: in the cave carved out behind the rock covered in birds, and unfortunately, their crap. Though the sand within the cave is soft enough, she's made two beds from large fallen palm fronds and lies on one. I gather she's resting because her eyes are closed.

Somehow, she managed to find a handcart. In it, she stored several large plastic bags emblazoned with the banking event's logo.

I look inside. They're filled with containers of fresh fruit and pastries—the leftovers of the bankers' last meal —in this case, not the proverbial supper that disintegrated when the bomb went off but a continental breakfast. Yulia was also able to procure a case of unopened water bottles.

Hearing my footsteps, her eyes open and her terror turns to relief—

Until she hears me whisper, "Emmanuel is the terrorist."

Yulia sighs. "I suspected as much."

"How?… And why?"

"Because of what Tisa said."

"You knew her?… But she was dead before you got here!"

Yulia shakes her head. "I flew into Tanzania three days before the cyclone hit. My true purpose was to obtain a *pension alimentaire*—what you call a palimony severance agreement. It would have finalized my relationship with Alain Micheaux. Little did I know Alain would also be here for the bankers' forum!" She sighs, disgusted. "It is why I stayed out of sight. Otherwise, he would have tried to convince me to call off the *alimentaire*, and my undercover investigation of his financial dealings would be null and void. You see, my purpose on the island was to formally sever my relationship with Alain, who I'd been investigating for embezzlement."

"You were investigating *your partner?*"

"Yes, for TRACFIN. I'm an undercover field operative. They knew his financial dealings were suspect. He advertised for a personal assistant. I was chosen to infiltrate because I am his type." She tosses her long blond hair. "As in such cases, getting closer means relenting to his insistence on an intimate relationship." She shrugs. "In my country, it is…how do you Americans say it?… Ah, yes, 'par for the course.'"

"In other words, your legal system doesn't consider it entrapment."

"If that were the case, half of all indictments in France would be thrown out of court." Yulia rolls her eyes. "*Mon ami*, the French invented the term 'agent provocateur.' Still, I find it more apropos that it is better known as a lingerie brand."

"You were the operative Jack met a few years back when you were undercover." I can't help but laugh. "You certainly had me fooled! I guess your Russian accent threw me off."

Yulia rolls her eyes. "My parents immigrated from Russia to France when I was an infant—all the more reason I felt the need to give back to our chosen country. I'd formerly been a model and can claim a White Russian heritage." She shrugs. "For TRACFIN, it is the perfect background for a covert operative. How was it so colorfully described to me?… Oh yes! As a Eurotrash party animal gold digger."

"Those were Jack's words, not mine," I insist.

Yulia rolls her eyes. "Yes, I know. When Jack finally came face to face with me in my cabana—*with the flimsy excuse of delivering extra towels*—he teased me that my cover has never been flattering." She smirks. "The pot should not call the kettle black."

I put my cards on the table: "He stayed the night with you."

"Purely innocent. After we put on a show for those who may have been listening, he fell asleep."

I'm ashamed to admit I may have been one of the eavesdroppers.

She continues: "He was so tired! I didn't have the heart to wake him. He left at five that morning. I'd mentioned my suspicions about Sabine." She shrugs. "He took his 'extra towels' to her cabana. He knew time was of the essence."

My heart is broken. I doubted him about Yulia, even though I know how much he despises playing the role of a raven.

Jack doesn't like using sex as a weapon any more than I do. Whereas it shames me, it makes him angry. We both take it out on our targets. But unlike me, he doesn't accuse me of enjoying it.

What makes him crazy is knowing I appreciate Lee's adoration. When we leave this godforsaken island, I'll do whatever is needed to prove I trust him—and to ensure he trusts me, too.

So that this critical conversation happens sooner than later, I ask: "How did you meet Tisa?"

Yulia closes her eyes as if she's watching the incident replay in her mind. "Before going to the resort, I thought it best to present my credentials as a TRACFIN operative to Inspector Salum. When Tisa knocked on Salum's door, he invited her in. It was obvious they were close friends. Salum had even mentioned a tip they'd received: that the banking event was to be infiltrated by terrorists. He asked her to keep her eyes open for anything that might verify the rumor. Upon hearing this, Tisa told

Salum that a new guest had arrived the day before: Oskar Surbeck. Salum then divulged that his investigators had noted that its captain had piloted the yacht from Nevis earlier that week. Emmanuel, who had been away on a business trip, also arrived that day, but he did so by ferry. One of Oskar's requests was that his concierge tidy his yacht and his cabana. When Tisa got to the dock, the yacht's name—Zero-Sum Game—took her by surprise. A month prior, she saw incorporation papers on Emmanuel's desk for a company. It was named Zero-Sum Game LLC and was based in Switzerland. As Tisa tidied Oskar's yacht, she noticed a statement from a Swiss bank for the same company. Oskar had carelessly left it in the yacht's study."

"She saw it as proof that they were in business together," I deduce.

"Yes. And here is the strangest part: Emmanuel pretended not to know him when Oskar arrived at the resort. Stymied, Tisa wrote down the bank account number on a tiny slip of paper. But then she heard Oskar whistling down the dock toward the yacht. Realizing he'd be there at any moment, Tisa hid the paper somewhere she thought he'd never look: in a metal cigar tube he'd tossed into the trash. But she was afraid to walk out with it for good reason. Oskar had already groped her." Yulia tears up. "She was so scared that she was shaking. Investigator Salum asked that I walk Tisa back to the ferry dock."

"If Emmanuel and Tisa were brother and sister, why didn't she speak with a Tanzanian accent?" I ask.

"It's the other way around," Yulia counters. "As Tisa

explained, they were born in Tanzania. Their family immigrated to the United States as infants and were fully Americanized. From a young age, Emmanuel's tech skills were how he leapfrogged academic grades. He was given a full scholarship to Georgia Tech, where he was first in his class for IT Security. While at university, he rarely wrote or called Tisa, let alone their parents. No matter. They were proud of him and thrilled that various firms had recruited him. He chose Oskar Surbeck's bank." Yulia sighs. "Tisa truly believed that Emmanuel was in over his head, and she was worried for him."

"What Tisa didn't know was that Emmanuel was Oskar's inside man for this massive scheme." I point out. "That, together, they'd plotted to hold the bank representatives captive, terrorize them, and then scan their eyes and force them to transfer their companies' funds to a master account established in Oscar's bank."

"That validates something I'd heard at TRACFIN before making my way here," Yulia says. "A rumor had taken the black-hat hacking community by storm about a hack tested on a financial institution. Like many in that industry, some of its executive suite personnel hold, and I quote, the keys to the kingdom. That is to say, their eye scans may unlock their institutions' electronic vault."

"What exactly is that?"

"As its name suggests, it is a way to move around the institution's financial assets, as well as those of its clientele."

"Ransomware?" I ask.

"No. Purely theft."

"Oskar and his tech genius, Emmanuel, were going to rob all the banks and stash the assets…where?"

Yulia smirks. "Who knows? Perhaps launder it. Art, real estate, etcetera. An unlimited bank account means unlimited purchasing power."

When I pick my mouth off the floor, I exclaim, "It would cause a worldwide depression!"

"Isn't that the point? They would have ruled the world." Yulia acknowledges. "But then the storm happened."

"And his sister's life was the first of their many casualties."

The irony of my response sobers her up. "I only found out about her death the following day. Investigator Salum summoned me from my hotel before I joined Rufus and his other clients on the yacht ride to Kisiwa Cha Paradiso. He informed me of Tisa's death just before he walked in to interrogate you." A tear runs down Yulia's cheek.

"So, it was you behind the two-way mirror!"

Yulia nods. "At that point, Investigator Salum didn't know you were an Acme operative. I left when he informed you that Interpol cleared you of any wrongdoing. I was rushing to join Rufus and his clients on the yacht. Had I missed it, I'd have blown my cover." She sighs. "Even knowing that you had a husband who, at that moment, was being investigated in another room, it never dawned on me that he was the same man I'd met years ago on another mission."

"Believe me, I also wish Rufus hadn't offered us a lift," I admit.

Yulia sighs. "I wonder how things would have turned out if I had missed the ride. Perhaps I'd have been able to get a call through to TRACFIN and inform it that the island was to be under siege by terrorists, no less ones led by Oskar Surbeck and Emmanuel Zuberi. By the time the yacht arrived, all communication had been cut off by the storm."

I shake my head in awe of our fates and those whose world we entered.

"When Jack came to your cabana, did you mention your suspicions about Emmanuel to him?"

"Yes. He found it hard to believe. Understandable. After all, Tisa was his sister. And up until then, Emmanuel had been cooperating with your investigation—"

Suddenly, we hear gunfire, and a lot of it—

Coming from the next lagoon over:

Lee's.

Does this mean Jack, Lee, and perhaps others are alive?

Have they been hiding there, and now have been discovered?

I run out.

Yulia is on my heels.

19

Volatility

In financial terms, "volatility" is a statistical measure of returns for a given security or market index. The measured financial instrument is considered volatile if the asset shows big swings, either high or low, from the market's standard deviation. If so, it is a crucial factor when pricing options contracts.

This term can be used in any situation.

A perfect example is desserts.

Suppose you're in a restaurant and your mouth is watering for the dark chocolate mousse cake described so ecstatically by your wait person. You'll be disappointed when she circles back to tell you she's just served the last piece to someone at the following table.

Does that mean you stomp over there and snatch it from under the nose of the lucky recipient? No—because you're not a child whose behavior is volatile.

Does this mean that such rudeness never occurs? Sadly, periodically, it is bound to happen! As the wait staff at any restaurant can attest, someone has reamed them out for just this situation. However, *the odds—that is, the market's standard deviation—are that it is rare.*

Still, the scout in you must be prepared for anything—including someone willing to swipe the last piece of your favorite restaurant's signature cake.

Ergo, a quick stab with the most miniature fork in your place setting (the one that allows you to look dainty as you eat fish) will make the point (no pun intended) quite well. Best yet, the puncture will be tiny enough that you can claim your innocence.

That's called having your cake and eating it too.

A crowbar. It's all I have.

It and the cover provided by sheets of rain falling from the sky and the attention of highly trained soldiers of fortune sharpshooters who are gunning at someone—*someones*—trying to get off the island.

If Jack is one of these someones, I pray he doesn't get hurt.

I pray the same for Lee. And also for Porter and the rest of those who serve and protect.

I pray that for me, too.

And yes, for Yulia, especially when I see she's not afraid to be fierce. She has snuck up to the first terrorist we see and cracks a coconut over his head. This allows us to take his M4 Carbine, night vision goggles, Glock, and a knife. Like those assigned to Acme, it's a hand-forged Alpha.

Yulia doesn't even blink when I slit his throat.

Jack is fighting for his life. I need him to know I am too.

And so it goes. A second terrorist's gunfire shows us his location. When I shoot him, it's from behind with one shot to the head with his dead friend's Glock.

We keep following the gunfire. The terrorists are so set on their mission—stopping the civilians from getting off the island before they can use their eyes to break into their banks' accounts—that they don't realize they've got us on their rear flank.

For us, it's down to guerrilla warfare. The terrorists are our prey.

At the same time, we make sure not to be seen by those who can do us harm.

It's not as if Emmanuel's army doesn't already have its hands full. The U.S. Navy sea base shooting back has an unfair advantage regarding personnel and munitions.

How did it get here so fast? Even out of office, does Lee still have that sort of clout?

If so, I must find out where he and Jack are hiding. The last thing I want is to miss the rigid-hull inflatable boat now skimming the storm-tossed waves toward Jack and the others under siege on the beach.

I point it out to Yulia. "Look! A RHIB is headed here."

She lights up but wonders: "Even if we get to the pick-up point, how will it know not to shoot at us, too?"

"Great question. The best way is for us to join the others before they're picked up by the boat headed their way."

She acknowledges the likelihood of my pipe dream

with a shrug. To her credit, she turns that frown upside down by sighting our next target and pulling the trigger.

All it takes is that one shot.

We run over, grab his munitions, and duck and dodge to our final destination.

Don't Jack and Lee realize someone is giving them much-needed cover? My god, this isn't Hogwarts! It's not as if they're wearing invisible coats.

Yulia motions me forward. "Look! The boat has reached the shore!"

She's right. It's still returning gunfire, giving the survivors much-needed coverage. There are still two assailants shooting at them. Each is on a different side of the opening to the beach. I scan the left side first, inch by inch.

Ah, there he is: high in a tree.

A shot to the chest slams him against its trunk. But he's not there for long. Hit by a high-velocity projectile, a body in motion stays in motion—

Even if it's a corpse.

Like Yulia, I'm now running through the brush—

And then I see him: the next terrorist on a mission to kill Jack and the others. He's high on a cliff. To make his shot, he must stand up but aim low.

I look to see who he's sighted:

It's Jack, who's now helping Sabine into the boat.

As the man's finger squeezes his gun's trigger—

I squeeze mine.

The bullet catapults him off the ledge—

He lands at Jack's feet.

Seeing this, someone screams: Akira. Her husband

picks her up and tosses her into the Navy boat, then tumbles in after her.

In seconds, everyone is scrambling on too: Xiāng, the bankers, Rufus, Sabine, and of course Lee, who waits until the innocent civilians are onboard before allowing Porter and the other agents to trundle him over the side.

As for Jack, his eyes scan the jungle beyond the beach, looking for his savior.

Doesn't he know it's me? Doesn't he hear me screaming his name now?

Doesn't he see me running to him?

But then I trip—

By the time Yulia pulls me back onto my feet, I'm dizzy and in pain.

And Jack has been coaxed onboard too, despite his determination to seek out their rescuer:

Me.

As the boat pulls away, the last thing I see before the storm shrouds Jack from view is Sabine huddling against him and looking into his face with adoring eyes.

I'm stubborn. I insist on waiting another ten minutes to see if Jack has convinced the boat to come for us.

It doesn't.

"Another ten," I insist to Yulia.

She tugs on my arm. "Please, Donna—we must go back to the cave! We've killed so many of the terrorists that by now Emmanuel must be wondering why they haven't come back to report on the skirmish."

She's right.

"Okay." I let her pull me along the sand. Finally, we get to the path that eventually breaks off to the one that will take us to the lagoon with our hidden cave—

When we come face to face with another terrorist.

He's just as surprised as us. But he's not so taken aback that he doesn't reach for his Glock and points it to the closest target: Yulia—

In a second, I've slipped my right hand behind his hairy wrist. At the same time, I grab the barrel of his gun with my left, wrenching it so hard and so fast and so high that I break his trigger finger—

And now I'm holding his gun.

I shoot him in the chest.

At least it puts him out of his misery—

And shuts him up.

Though he's fallen clear of the path and into the undergrowth, I still feel the urge to kick him. Yes. I'm that angry, and it feels. So good that I do it again and again.

I don't care that his guts spill out, spattering my leg. I don't care that Yulia is begging me to get ahold of myself.

Her words finally sink in when she mutters, "Someone else is coming!"

At that point, I duck with her beside a mangrove tree.

When the next guy comes into view, my kill shot is to the heart. He crumples backward into the brush.

Yulia is heaving. When she stops, she wipes her mouth with the back of her hand. Then she grabs the legs of this dead guy and drags him deeper into the foliage. When he's well hidden, she heads to our cave.

I'm calm enough—make that smart enough—to keep my mouth shut and follow her.

But I take the heartless guy's gun, too.

Yulia doesn't speak along the way. Instead, she grabs fallen branches, which I guess is to make a fire so that we'll keep warm tonight.

I follow her lead.

When we get to the cave, she signals me to go in. Sure, I don't mind being the sitting duck. I guess I owe it to her.

Seeing we're in the clear, I motion her in. For the first half hour, we feast silently on fruit and pastries. Finally, she says, "At least Rufus got away too."

"Speaking of Rufus…" I come out with it: "The blind banker, Claudio, was seated on a plane in the row in front of three of the terrorists. He described one as a male and American. Jack thought he meant Rufus."

Yulia snickers. "I guess that by now, Jack knows his assumption was wrong. Rufus is a CIA asset as well as one for TRACFIN. We've worked together on numerous ops. As a divorce lawyer for wealthy soon-to-be ex-wives who are privy to their husbands' financial shenanigans, his intel is appreciated by both organizations. Rufus and I arrived earlier than his other clients. While I watched your interrogation, he secured the private yacht and its captain. He had no idea who Jack or you were. Otherwise, I'd have stopped him from inviting you along—and why I stayed out of sight."

"Another voice was described as male and British. Since Tisa verified that Oskar and Emmanuel came to the island on the same day, though he's Swiss, I now realize Oskar's perfect British accent makes him the most likely suspect."

"When did Claudio arrive on the island?" Yulia asks.

"He'd already been here two weeks before the conference started," I reply. Because of his blindness, he gives himself extra time to acclimate to the climate, the surroundings, and the serenity. He loves—well, he loved it here. He called it the antithesis of Madrid."

"He validates what Tisa said—that he arrived around the same time as Emmanuel," Yulia points out. "You came in a week later. By the way, when did you first meet Emmanuel?"

"The day we discovered Tisa's body in our lagoon. As you heard me tell Investigator Salum, Jack and I met her when we arrived because she'd been our concierge. But we never saw her afterward because we opted for seclusion. All requested items were left in the dumbwaiter."

"By the time you found Tisa, she'd been in the water for over twelve hours. Someone else was servicing your requests."

I sit up. "It was Emmanuel."

"How do you know?"

"Because when we asked about Tisa, I could tell he was uncomfortable discussing her. Also, he claimed she'd gone to the mainland for a family emergency."

"We now know he is an atrocious liar," Yulia murmurs.

I hesitate, but then I come out with it: "I had you detained by Porter because Claudio described the third conspirator as female and Slavic. I assumed it was you."

This gives her cause to laugh. "You had me detained because you were jealous of what you perceived as Jack's lust for me."

"You're right," I concede. "And I'm sorry about that."

"Apology accepted." She shrugs. Admittedly, I'd have been the most likely suspect if I hadn't arrived a few days before you. Your husband can vouch for my credentials." She leans in. There is another person who fits that description. She is also Rufus's client. Can you guess?"

"Don't leave me in suspense." Especially when I'm filthy, tired, and aching, and a box of croissants is within inhaling distance.

"Sabine Dubois, of course."

"But she's French! ...Isn't she?"

"She is a French national, *oui*. However, the DGSE—France's Direction Générale de la Sécurité Extérieure — suspects her of being a Russian operative," Yulia explains. When I divulged this to Jack, he knew cavorting with Sabine was the most optimum use of his time."

"He was right." Jack did his duty despite my jealousy. I shake my head at my stupidity.

And now he's sailing away—with her.

Whereas I'm stuck here.

As long as Emmanuel and his thugs don't find me.

"So, what shall we do next?" Yulia wonders aloud.

She's asking me?

Ah, hell. This keeps getting better.

"We sleep," I reply. "Tomorrow, we get up early and try to get off this hellhole of an island."

The birds are going crazy outside of our cave.

I don't take that as a good sign.

They wake up Yulia, too.

Frightened, she now scrambles for an M4.

I do the same, but it's too late:

A dark figure stands over me, shouldering both guns.

"Get up—*now*."

I know that voice:

Jack's.

20

Safe Haven Demand

*T*his term describes the difference between Treasury bonds and stock returns over the three weeks of trading days. In volatile times, bonds do better when investors are scared.

Investors use such assets to limit their exposure during times of market instability. Believe it or not, there's something called a "Fear & Greed Index," which uses increasing safe-haven demand as a signal for fear.

Think of your safe haven demand as that one item in your closet that's your go-to in good times and bad: for example, when you don't have the time or the money to shop for a new outfit—

Especially when you need to cover the few extra pounds you're packing.

~

Jack?...

"You're here!" I exclaim. "But… how?"

He nods indifferently. "And you're alive."

"Are you surprised?"

Or, say, ecstatic that I survived the explosion?

Maybe you're relieved you don't have to bring what's left of me back to the kids in a body bag?

Anything?

"Frankly, no. I could tell by the kill shots that, in all likelihood, you were covering our flank." Nonchalantly, he adds, "You'll be relieved to know that the captives who survived are now safely aboard the Expeditionary Sea Base USS Hershel Woody Williams. Thankfully, it was already in the area since it was scheduled to participate in a multinational maritime exercise with Tanzania and some of our other partner nations in this region. The cyclone put a kibosh on that. The Williams' Captain let me borrow a RHIB to retrieve those we left behind."

"It's good to see you." Surely, he hears the relief in my voice.

And yet his eyes register nothing. "I'd hoped you had Claudio with you," Jack grimaces. "Other than you and Yulia, he was the only living civilian who didn't make it off the island."

"My god! No one helped him out?"

Jack nods. "Gretta was assigned to guide him. But when the terrorists entered the keynote dinner, she was on the other side of the room as the lights went out. Like the others, she panicked."

Do you have any indication that Claudio is still alive?" Yulia asks.

"The terrorists—or what's left of them—claim he's their prisoner. For his return, they're requesting a ransom and safe passage. If the terrorists don't get their way by sunrise, all bets are off. A SEAL team is on its way, but it's doubtful it will arrive in time."

"By that, you mean Emmanuel will kill Claudio," I reply.

Jack nods. His eyes shift to Yulia. "You mentioned Tisa's suspicions about Emmanuel. Sadly, she was right."

"Still, I'm sure Sabine did her best to lead you in the wrong direction," Yulia murmurs.

Better this supposition comes from her than from me.

"Let me put it this way: Sabine insisted her visit to the island was purely personal," Jack admits. "And when I searched her cabana, there was nothing to indicate she was there for any other purpose than her divorce."

"When she dropped the electronic pad before entering the banking event, I knew something was up. And by the way, Rufus was suspicious of her, too." I know I should leave it at that, but I can't help but rub it in: "I tried to warn you about her, Jack. But you wouldn't listen."

"If memory serves me, you were jealous of Yulia too." Jack retorts. "Let's just say you're not the most credible witness when you're in that state of mind, shall we?"

I huff, "Says the man who bristles for no reason every time Lee is around!"

"Do you really want to go there?" Jack snaps.

"Enough, you two!" Yulia shouts. "Mérde! Such mêlées are why I will never marry!" She shrugs. "For love, that is."

"The fact Sabine ran for her life must indicate she wasn't in cahoots with Emmanuel," Jack points out.

I snicker. "You presume too much. Her escape may

have been all for show. Had the cyclone not rolled in and blown the terrorists' mission to hell and a handbasket, she'd be with Emmanuel right now."

Jack shrugs. "How many did you take out?"

He's trying to change the subject, but I'll take it as a mea culpa. "Six."

From Jack's slight smile, I know he's impressed.

"By now, they may have found the bodies of those we took out, so they'll suspect an adversary or two never got off the island," I reason. "They'll hunt us down."

"Capturing a few more hostages—especially if they're women—would give Emmanuel even more leverage," Jack points out. "Same with me, so we can't let that happen. Sneak attacks are the order of the day."

When Jack steps to one side, we see he's brought a gunnysack. He pulls out three tactical kits. While he hands them out, he speaks directly to Yulia: "You'll be kitted up with some essentials: LED flashlight, night vision goggles, and a lighter. You'll carry Sigs with suppressors and ammo. Since we'll have to split up, you also have an encrypted two-way radio. When the time comes, we can communicate with the Williams' commanding officer via encrypted satellite phones." Finally, Jack glances my way. "Any idea which cabanas the terrorists are in?"

"None," I admit. "Our game plan was to attack when confronted. Otherwise, we planned to keep our heads low until the cavalry showed up and to be near water when it did. The terrorists were posing as concierges, so they could still be in the employee barracks. But if I'm to give an educated guess, I'd say that they've spread out so they can see an attack from all angles."

"They'll have a guard with Claudio at all times, so that keeps one man from sentry duty," Jack reasons.

"Now that the cyclone is moving away, we won't have as much cover," Yulia points out.

"We have one thing working in our favor." Jack grins. He's being coy—for Yulia's sake, not mine.

"Oh? And what's that?" I ask.

Jack takes me by the shoulders and shoves me backward about four steps.

As if I'm going to let him bully me around!

Before I can shove back, he crouches down—

And brushes away the sand with his hand.

A metal hatch is revealed. Jack lifts a protruding handle, revealing what lies beneath it: a stone stairwell.

Even with a flashlight, I can't see where it ends.

"Tunnels will certainly give us an advantage," Yulia points out.

"How did you know this was here?" I ask. "And where does it lead?"

"It's how I got into the cave without you seeing me. It's one of a series of tunnels. They crisscross the island. As for who discovered it, we can thank Porter. He's an avid history buff. Before he goes anywhere new, he reads about it. In his research about Kisiwa Cha Paradiso, he found a book on Zanzibar's history of slavery spanning a thousand years. It went on until the early 1900s. To hide, runaway slaves created a series of tunnels on Paradiso. Before this trip, Porter mentioned it to Lee and suggested that the security team map them out in case an emergency exit was needed."

"Talk about prescience!" I exclaim. "Is this how you got Lee and the others out during the terrorists' bedlam?"

Jack nods. "Gretta informed Lee's security detail that the event cabana had a riser beneath the stage. At one point, it had been an orchestra pit for theatrical productions. One of the tunnel's stairwells opens into it. When the shooting started, while some of Lee's agents returned fire, the others secured Lee's getaway and then helped as many of the bankers as possible through the tunnel closest to the Williams. Most of the tunnels have openings on nearby lagoons or beaches." Jack frowns. "Sadly, Lee lost one of his agents."

I bow my head. Through the years, I'd met them all. "I'm sorry to hear that." Thank God it wasn't Porter! Aunt Phyllis would have been as traumatized as the rest of us who know and love him.

"The tunnels are as sprawling as an ant farm," Jack continues. "They pop up in caves within reach of the beach like this one and in practically every corner of the forest. When the cabanas were originally built in the 1920s, many of the formerly enslaved or their descendants were still alive and worked on the construction teams. Since they knew they'd also be hired to staff the resort as servants, they figured out they could more quickly service the resort's clientele if they built discreet doors in closets, pantries, and basements that accessed the tunnels. This was done in several of the larger buildings, including the one that became the event cabana, Lee's cabana, and some of the larger historic cabanas."

"Surely Emmanuel must know about these," Yulia marvels.

Jack shakes his head. "When Porter first went through the tunnels, he could tell they hadn't been used in decades. Prudently, he never brought it up with Emmanuel. It may have been to protect one of Lee's many pipe dreams: to buy the island outright and use it as the headquarters for his World Peace and Prosperity Initiative."

"Sounds like a project he'd love," I reply.

"You should know," Jack mutters.

Yulia's head spins from me to him and back to me as if she's watching a fast and furious tennis match. Sadly, the type of points being scored doesn't move us closer to love.

Game, set, match—

Divorce.

"What should we do now?" This is Yulia's way of changing the subject.

"We have a two-fold mission," Jack replies. "The priority is finding Claudio. The tunnels will help tremendously. And so will these little gadgets." He pulls out a small handheld device with a screen. "It's a DensePose scanner. Unlike infrared thermography—which only registers heat-emitting forms but doesn't penetrate solid barriers like walls, concrete, or brick—anyone holding an emitting WiFi-enabled device will appear on its screen. They look like digital ghosts."

"*Ingénieuse,*" Yulia murmurs.

"Agreed. Three geniuses at Carnegie Mellon invented it. This is the prototype. The US Military is testing it," Jack explains.

"Even with this, how will we know if we've found Claudio or if it's one of the terrorists?" I ask.

"We won't, for two reasons. Unlike an infrared scanner, the DensePose shows the device's user. However, it doesn't pick up heat that may be in the walls surrounding the person. Instead, we'll have to use deductive reasoning," Jack admits. "I'm spitballing here, but a solitary person in a small room that could be a cell would be my bet. There may be a second person nearby. One or both may be stationary, which could indicate a captive."

"Got it," Yulia murmurs.

"So, what's the other part of our mission?" I ask.

Jack holds up two small disks. "These are GPS trackers. Ideally, on or before sunrise—which occurs at oh-six-twenty-four this morning, an F22 will release two precision-guided missiles in the hope that at least one will blow Emmanuel—and anyone near him—sky-high once and for all." He tosses one to me and the other to Yulia. "Donna, you should put it in Emmanuel's cabana. Yulia, your disk should be placed in his office. Hiding it in anything he might wear would be ideal so that, God willing, one of the missiles doesn't miss." Jack looks at his watch. "It's already after four. In less than two hours, all bets are off." Jack points down into the tunnel. "Time's a-wasting. After you, ladies."

21

The Last Mile

While online, you see something you'd like to buy: say, a silk blouse.

And low and behold—it's on sale!

You choose a flattering color—pink, of course.

And huzzah! The retailer has it in your size.

Even better: delivery is free without a minimum purchase amount in your cart.

And here's the best news: they can have it on your doorstep tomorrow.

To economists, the term "last mile" summarizes complex and costly analyses for the providers of goods and services to densely populated areas.

It isn't an easy task! There are a lot of people involved in getting your blouse from Point A (a store or warehouse) to Point B (wrapped and packed) to Point C (picked up or delivered by the first mode of transportation needed; perhaps a truck?) to Point D (handed off to a plane) to Point E (another warehouse) to Point F (another truck) to your front door.

In essence, you are a cottage industry.

No—make that a global industry. Because someone somewhere owns a silkworm farm (China?) where the silk was harvested.

And somewhere else is the factory that took the silk yarn to make the material for your blouse.

And somewhere else, a factory made the buttons.

And then someone designed the blouse for the factory that sewed it—

Just for you.

Think of all the people who have jobs just because you need to look pretty.

Don't let them down! Keep buying!

We follow Jack into the dark, dank tunnel. From what I can tell, he's right. The tunnels haven't been used in quite some time. Creepy crawlers—giant spiders, beetles, even a few snakes—skitter away when hit with our flashlight beams or feel the vibrations from our footsteps. Yulia yelps when a mouse runs over her toes.

Because I'm the first to turn the next corner, I get a face full of spider web that has me gagging and choking.

Jack laughs.

I resist the urge to punch him.

Yulia slaps Jack's shoulder. *"Ferme ta gueule!"*

He rolls his eyes, but I see no need to stick out my tongue now that he's been duly chastised.

In time, we get to the three-way split on Jack's maps. Jack turns to me. "You'll use the tunnel in the middle. It comes out closest to Emmanuel's cabana. He may have guards, so plant the GPS disk, then get the hell out. Understand?"

I nod.

Jack continues: "I'll take the tunnel on the right, which should put me on the far side of the men's concierge cabanas. It may be where they're holding Claudio. Even if it isn't, they may be sleeping in shifts there. I'll take out as many as possible." Jack's eyes shift to Yulia. "You'll take the tunnel on the left. It should put you underneath Emmanuel's office. You can leave the disk there, preferably on his desk or secreted in something he's left there to wear. But remember: securing Claudio is priority number one. If it turns out that I'm wrong and you find Claudio there instead, don't enter alone. Call us so we can provide backup. Either Donna or I, or both, can terminate his captors while you help him to the tunnel and guide him to the RHIB. However, if there's less than a half hour on the clock and we haven't gotten to you, don't wait around. Take Claudio to the Williams in the RHIB while Donna and I ensure Emmanuel has at least one of the disks."

She nods and takes off.

Don't wait around.

In other words, Jack and I will be on the island when the missiles blow it up.

"Until death do we part" may be in our future after all.

It'll be a memorable vacation, alright—but for all the wrong reasons.

My tunnel climbs steadily up the island's central hill. Finally, I see a few digital ghosts: about five. Each walks off in a different direction. I take it that they are on patrol.

Instead of engaging, I text Jack with their coordinates.

Finally, I get to the tunnel that ends inside Emmanuel's cabana. My heart leaps when I see a digital ghost.

He's home.

It lies prone. I wait a minute for any movement. None. He must be sleeping.

A second ghost is there, sitting straight up but far enough away that it could be one of Emmanuel's men guarding his cabana.

The tunnel ends at a stairwell close to Emmanuel's position. I climb to the door but find it bolted. I try to turn it, but it won't budge.

I shove the bolt with all my might. That does the trick. It creaks open—

Into darkness. I peek through:

I'm in a beautiful library. A massive ornate desk, facing out, is the focal point of one wall. An oversized chair and credenza sit behind it. Two other walls are floor-to-ceiling bookcases. A third wall has a picture window over built-in bookshelves topped by a wide ledge. A settee, placed in the middle of the room, faces the picture window.

The cabana sits atop a hill. The night sky is still too

cloudy to see the lush green jungle below it, but I can hear waves still crazed by the last vestiges of the cyclone crashing onto the beach.

I scan the office. Emmanuel has quite a wall of fame. Behind his desk are pictures of him with various dignitaries and celebrities.

I'm not surprised to see a photo of him with Oskar. Younger and in suits, their backdrop is Lucern's Mount Pilatus.

Well, isn't that hilarious! Emmanuel managed to get a photo with Lee before he tried to kill him. I'd take it with me if I had a darker sense of humor, though I don't think Lee would appreciate the memento.

In another photo on Emmanuel's desk, he's twelve, or maybe ten. Tisa, younger and smaller, sits beside him. They have their arms around each other.

Money makes the world go round.

And to crash and burn.

Not if I plant the GPS disk where it can do the most harm.

What would he take that he'd always have on him? His cell or his wallet is a given. They are probably on his dresser in his bedroom. The former would have no place to hide the disk. The latter would be risky, too. There is no guarantee he'd wear a specific jacket or pair of pants.

Then it hits me: his John Lobb penny loafers.

I open the library door and look out onto a hallway. No one is there. Silently, I pass an open door to another bedroom. It's empty, and it's not the master.

The next room is a bathroom.

Across the way is another bedroom with an ensuite bath.

The last door is at the very end of the hall. When I reach it, I twist the knob slowly, praying that it won't creak and give me away. I open it just wide enough to look in:

Emmanuel snores on the kingsized bed. A set of double doors is to one side. They open inward.

I slip into the room and go over to the large walk-in closet. Bespoke suits and jackets take up a whole wall. Another holds slacks. A wall of shelves displays clear boxes of paired shoes.

For a resort manager, he's spending his hard-stolen money as if he were a wolf of Wall Street.

Next to the mirror, an ornate valet rack holds the clothes he's picked out for the morning. I look at the labels. The shirt, turquoise linen, is Turnbull & Asser. It's paired with a gray multi-checked linen blend Barrington blazer and charcoal trousers.

He'll notice if I put it in one of the blazer's pockets and he puts his hand in it. The same goes for trousers. I look down at the John Lobb penny loafers. I could replace the penny in the left loafer's band with the GPS disk. But will Emmanuel notice?

Perhaps I'll leave the penny where it is. Instead, I can tuck the tracker under the far side of the band.

I'm just about to do this when my two-way radio chirps.

I freeze. Quickly, I turn off the device. I'll turn it back on once I'm safe.

The snoring stops—

But then Emmanuel's cell buzzes.

He groans, then reaches for it.

"What is it?… Ah! *Another captive?* Well done! I'll meet you at the door."

I hear movement. He's getting out of bed.

Footsteps come my way.

Before Emmanuel steps into the closet, I duck into the bathroom. Silently, I step into the shower stall. The glass is fluted. Still, I press down and low against the back tile wall.

And just in time. Naked, he enters, lifts the toilet seat, and relieves himself.

I pray he doesn't shower next.

Instead, he goes into the closet. Damn it, he's getting dressed.

As quietly as I can, I walk out. Gently, I close the door behind me. Then I run down the hall to the library.

I wait until I'm safely in the tunnel and at the intersection of where we started before turning on the two-way radio.

The call was from Jack. "Good news. Claudio is with me. But listen, they beat him badly. He can't even walk."

"Will he survive?"

"Yes. No internal wounds. But I've got to carry him back to the RHIB. I'm in the tunnel now headed that way."

"Any enemy casualties?"

"Three." Jack's heaving indicates he's moving pretty fast despite having Claudio on his back. "Any movement on your part?"

"Yes…and no. When you called, I was in the middle of planting the GPS on Emmanuel."

"Did you succeed?" he asks.

"That's the 'no' part."

"Shit!"

I wince at his disappointment. I didn't want to let him down.

"I was about to do it, but a phone call woke him up," I explain. "He mentioned something about 'another captive' and then got up to get dressed—"

"Ah, hell! But…who?…" His voice trails off. "Have you heard from Yulia?"

"No." Dread surges through me. "Maybe a banker you thought was dead survived after all—"

"Call her, Donna. If she answers, tell her I have Claudio and to head to the beach as soon as possible. If she doesn't answer…" His voice trails off.

I know what he's thinking.

"Take care of Claudio, Jack. I promise Yulia and I will meet you there."

Jack sighs, and then he signs off. He gets the message: I won't leave unless she's with me.

I call Yulia.

No answer.

I try again.

Again, no answer.

Perhaps, like me, she's gone radio silent because she's worried about being picked up by bad guys.

I wait until I've reached the tunnel she took. It's narrower than mine and Jack's and lower in height. Also, it circles a narrow bend.

This time, she picks up.

Only it's not her. A man's voice says, "Mrs. Craig? I have her. Tell the powers that be that the deal is the same."

The phone goes dead.

I recognize the voice from the banker's event: it's that of the lead captor:

Jolly Green Giant.

22

Margin Call

An investor may feel the need to open a margin account. It contains some combination of the investor's money and some borrowed from the broker.

If the account's equity value hasn't risen to the minimum value indicated by the account's maintenance requirement over a specific time, a "margin call" will be initiated. At that point, the investor has a choice: (a) provide additional funds or securities, or (b) sell some of the assets already in the account.

It is genuinely a high-stakes crap shoot.

If margin calls make you feel like a frog in a pot on a flame that seems hotter than you'd like, follow this rule: if you can't stand the heat, get out of the kitchen.

~

Proof of life:

That's what I need right now.

I call back. Jolly Green picks up laughing raucously.

"Put her on," I demand.

Silence.

Finally: "Donna...I'm... so sorry." Yulia's dread weighs down every word.

"Are you still in or around Emmanuel's office?"

"*Oui.*"

Hearing her answer, I grab my kit and take off.

Because the building is much closer to the three-way split, and the tunnel is shorter and much narrower than the other three, it shouldn't take me long to reach the end of it. "I have your back," I reply. "Tell me: mission accomplished?"

"*Oui.*"

"Are you inside?"

"*Non.*"

"In front of the building?"

"*Oui.*"

"Good. Now, listen up: no matter where they tell you to go, once you are out of their sight, run as fast as you can to the path that puts you on the beach where Jack has anchored the RHIB. He's already there with Claudio. Got that?"

"*Oui.*"

"Super. Now Put *Reuze Papa of Casselon* back on the line." She snickers at my reference to the traditional carnival figures revered in Northern France.

I hear the hand-off. Then: "What is it, bitch?"

"Different deal. We do a swap. Me for her."

Again, silence.

The seconds turn into minutes: time I don't have to give.

Neither does he, but far be it from me to be the bearer of that bad news.

I use his hesitation to get to the end of the tunnel. I climb the stairwell. Its door opens a hatch on the basement floor in Emmanuel's office. I climb out. The basement door is unlocked, so I take the steps to Emmanuel's reception room.

No one is inside.

From the front window, I see Yulia. Her hands are cuffed. Two thugs guard her. Jolly Green and three other guys stand apart, scanning in different directions.

For signs of me, I suppose.

Finally, Jolly Green replies into Yulia's two-way radio: "Sure, okay. It's a deal."

"Tell her to walk toward the path leading to the airstrip," I tell him. "No escort. I'm on my way to you now."

Smirking, he motions two of the thugs to go in that direction. They think they'll ambush me.

Jolly Green gives a high sign to one of the guys guarding Yulia. When the man tries to gag her, she struggles but stops when he puts his gun to her head. "Take her to the boss man," Jolly Green commands. "The sadist is drooling to have his fun with her."

The thug marches her off in the direction of Emmanuel's cabana.

Shit.

I open a window just wide enough to put a bullet in the back of her captor.

When he drops, she takes off running.

His buddy runs after her.

At the same time, Jolly Green and the other three guys have turned their firepower on me. All the while, Jolly Green motions his thugs to circle the building.

I shoot off enough rounds to get them to think twice about his idea, but I see the writing on the wall:

I've got to get out of there, and fast.

I take off down the hallway, then detour into the basement.

They get inside just as I reach the tunnel hatch. I try to open it, but the hinges are rusty. I heave it open with all my might.

I've just climbed down, and I'm closing the hatch when someone walks into the basement: Jolly Green. With a roar, he runs over.

Quickly, I bolt it. Still, he grabs the handle and pulls with all his might but curses when he realizes it's locked. By the time he starts shooting a steady barrage of bullets, I'm far enough away that I miss getting hit by the ones that make it through the thick wooden hatch.

His handiwork has done enough damage that he can claw at the hatch's hinges with a crowbar, which means he and his buddies will be down here any moment.

I'm ready.

Slowly, Jolly Green lifts the hatch.

He hears nothing.

All he sees is darkness.

As far as he knows, I'm dead.

He finds out he's wrong when I pull the pin on one of my grenades and toss it up.

It goes high enough that, when the bit of a spin I put

on it kicks in, it arches to one side instead of falling back through the hole—

And lands on the basement floor with a hard *thunk*.

As I'd hoped, Jolly Green's first instinct is to close the hatch.

Which I then lock—

And run like hell.

I've just reached the main tunnel when I hear the explosion. Its vibration shakes the ground so violently that a whirling dervish of bats follows me as far as the intersection to all four—now three—passageways.

The bats go one way, and I go another.

I think they've come to the conclusion I'm lousy company.

It's Emmanuel's time to find that out, too.

23

Stocks and Bond(age)

Each unit of a stock, called a share, represents ownership in a company. Stocks, owned directly or through a mutual fund or ETF, will likely form most of an investor's portfolio.

Bonds are lower-risk and lower-return investments than stocks, which makes them an essential component of a balanced investment portfolio, especially for more conservative investors.

You'll also find stocks and other forms of bondage in any S&M club. These implements bind you so that you can receive pain.

Think of it as a bear market, but leaving permanent scars.

❧

I run through the tunnel under the stairwell that opens up in Emmanuel's library. I duck when I see a guard through the window. He's circling the cabana. In time, I open the door and look out into the hallway. No one is there, but I hear a slap followed by Yulia's anguished cry.

The sound comes from the master bedroom. This time, the door is wide open.

As silently as possible, I make my way down the hall. I hear Emmanuel before I see him and Yulia.

"If you wish to live, bitch, you better plead with me to spare your life," he snarls.

"You and I both know TRACFIN will pay your ransom to get me back," she retorts. "However, if you're looking for a reason to kill time, why don't I tell you what I know about you instead?"

"What the hell do you mean by that?" he roars.

"Tisa told me everything."

"*Tisa?*… You've… You've never met her!" Doubt colors his declaration.

"I did, in fact—*before your partner, Oskar Surbeck, killed her.*" Already woozy with pain, Yulia slurs her words.

Emmanuel is silent. He knows where she's going with this fascinating tale that rivets me.

"You'd been close as children. When you came back to Tanzania—specifically, here, to manage Kisiwa Cha Paradiso, she thought you'd found your true purpose. She'd hoped you and she could be close again."

Her words earn her another lash. The crack of his whip is punctuated with her scream.

"Why did she tell you this?" he demands.

"Because she wanted to stop you! She loved you, and didn't want you to get in trouble."

Emmanuel shouts, "Shut up, you bitch!" I hear another slash of a lash.

By now, I've reached the bedroom. I'm horrified by what I see:

Yulia is naked and seated backward on an upholstered chair. Her head and shoulders hang over the back of it. Her wrists are in cuffs tethered to a hook on the floor, and her ankles are strapped to its back legs, forcing her to extend her back.

In other words, she is essentially immobile.

She faces me, so I can't see the condition of her back. But the anguish in her face and the sprays of blood on the carpet speak volumes.

Emmanuel has laid out other instruments of torture on a stainless steel rolling table: knives and picks of varying sizes, pliers, and a blowtorch.

Jolly Green wasn't joking when he called Emmanuel a sadist.

Well, hey, no surprise there.

Emmanuel is so fixated on his task that he doesn't notice I've sidled by the door.

To save her, I have to get him away from there.

Taking a fistful of her hair, he jerks it up. "If you want to stay alive, tell me everything my sister said— *now.*"

I watch as he cups Yulia under her chin so she has to look at him. She groans from the pain. But because she knows she has something he wants, suddenly she smiles up at him, unafraid, and declares, "Tisa told me she'd seen the incorporation papers for the company you shared with him, Zero-Sum Game, which you'd left on your desk. Then Oskar showed up here in the yacht with that name. He asked her, his concierge, to tidy it up. As she did so, she saw Zero-Sum Game LLC's bank account statement. He'd callously left it on the counter. Concerned, she wrote down the account number. But he returned before leaving with it, so she hid it. She promised to come back the next day with extra towels." Yulia's voice tightens with anger. "Tisa didn't know the phrase was an offer to sexually service him. And she certainly didn't know he was a sadist. *But you did*—and you didn't warn her! She was *your sister!*"

Even Emmanuel shudders. He's thinking of his mentor's rough-sex antics.

She glances at Emmanuel's torture table. "I see he taught you his dating tips."

Her taunt earns her another stripe.

Yulia screams out. And yet, she refuses to be silenced: "She fought to get off the yacht, but he overpowered her, shackled her, and had his way with her And then he strangled her—reason enough to steer his yacht to another lagoon in the hope of dumping her body far enough away that he wouldn't be implicated. Unfortunately, he chose a lagoon with a reef ragged enough to rip a hole in his boat. He swam away, leaving her tied to the anchor." Yulia grins up at him. "She told me where she hid it."

Emmanuel demands, "Tell me as if your life depends on it because it does." He moves to the table. "Tell me! Where is it?"

Yulia's head is so pained that it lolls to one side. Still, she snickers, "After I tell you, I'm a dead woman."

He scoffs. "Even in this pathetic condition, you are still worth something to TRACFIN—though I doubt you'll be so enticing to your suspects after I'm done with you."

Emmanuel picks up the knife, scorches it with the blowtorch, and then presses the hot blade against her back.

Her scream sends chills down my spine.

"Tell me where it is!" he shouts.

"She… She hid it in… It's in an aluminum cigar tube." Yulia can barely be heard between her sobs.

The cigar tube is still on the boat.

Realizing this, too, Emmanuel's furious howl rings through the cabana.

Yulia raises her head—

And looks directly at me—

And smiles.

He follows her gaze—

To me, watching in the doorway.

His eyes meet mine.

I run out the door and down the hall as fast as possible to the library. I'm headed for the tunnel that will take me closest to where I need to be:

The boat resting at the bottom of my lagoon.

24

Zero-Sum Game

In any financial transaction, you need a seller and a buyer.

Ideally, the buyer will purchase the asset at a fair price. But sometimes the seller will take a loss. The transaction follows Isaac Newton's Third Law of Relativity in Physics: "For every action, there is an equal and opposite reaction."

In the financial universe, this is an example of what is meant by "Zero-Sum Game."

Often cited in game theory—in this case, options and futures—it simply means that one individual's gain is the equivalent of another's loss.

In other words, there is no net change in wealth because someone else loses for every person who gains on a contract.

Zero. Nada. Nothing.

In fact, there are two winners because you can't forget your broker's commissions. Cha-ching!

~

Because Emmanuel doesn't know how I entered his cabana, he also won't know where the tunnel emerges on land.

Thankfully, it's further away than he'd suspect.

Unfortunately for me, he's closer to the trail leading back to my lagoon, and he may get there first.

So instead, I run through the tunnel and detour to the one that will take me there the quickest.

I pause when I reach the trailhead where all paths crisscrossing this island begin. The last thing I want is to have him overtake me or to come up behind me and put a bullet in my back.

Then I remember rowboats are tethered to the dock of each cabana. I take the path to the inlet closest to ours: Flamingo Lagoon.

The storm destroyed Xiãng's dock. Its rowboat is capsized.

An uprooted tree crushed Yulia's cabana. Though her dock is still standing, the rowboat is nowhere to be found.

Windows in Sabine's cabana are shattered. The back end of its dock is gone, and its rowboat is capsized.

To my relief, Rufus's cabana still stands, as does its dock. However, his rowboat is floating in the lagoon.

I swim to it. My prayers are answered when I enter the boat and open the thwart. It still contains its two oars. Made of aluminum shafts, hard plastic blades screw on at one end and ribbed grips screw onto the other.

After clasping the oars into their crutch plates, I head for my inlet:

Happy Parrot Lagoon.

I row as if my life depends on it because it does, all the while praying that I'll get to the Zero-Sum Game first. If fate goes my way, I'll find the tube before Emmanuel arrives.

And then I try to remember the last time I was lucky.

At least not since this nightmare started.

In hindsight, I guess Jack choosing Kisiwa Cha Paradiso wasn't so lucky either.

But that's on him, not me.

Flamingo Lagoon is still as glass.

To my surprise, it has barely any damage: just the usual rubble of broken limbs and storm-tossed flora.

And yet, had I not known better, I have thought the last few days were all just a bad dream and that any moment Jack would appear on the deck with a couple of mojitos in hand to beckon me to his side.

Our solitude in paradise now feels like a million years ago.

When Tisa returned to the yacht for the cigar tube, Oskar may have never known her true reason for being there.

The tube may still be where she hid it.

There's only one way to find out.

I hide the rowboat on the far side of the now exposed outcropping that was the cause of Zero-Sum Game's demise. The side closest to the lagoon's mouth has ridges that jut sharply. The largest is several feet long. No wonder the damn yacht sank so quickly.

Oskar tied Tisa to the Zero-Sum Game's anchor, hoping she would decompose quickly while being ravaged by underwater tides and nibbled by sea creatures.

Had I lost my struggle with Oskar, what would he have done to my body?

Perhaps he would have left me here, too.

I take a deep breath and then dive into the dark lagoon.

Seven minutes is the longest I have ever held my breath underwater.

Will it be long enough to find where Tisa hid the aluminum tube?

The Zero-Sum Game is forty feet long. I spend Minute One in the main deck. The flask is not in any of the obvious places: the numerous drawers on the credenza beneath the fifty-five-inch TV monitor, all cabinets in the room, the now decaying tomes on the built-in bookcase, let alone stuck in or between the cushions tethered to the furniture. It's not in the club chairs, or the two facing L-shaped couches that are screwed into the beautiful marble floor. I don't find it in the built-in benches or the drawers of the gaming table. Nor is it hidden in the weighted chairs that surround the long rectangle dining table.

By Minute Two, I've moved on to the kitchen galley. As I open cabinets, items float out: condiment bottles, jars of spices, tins of caviar. Anything kept in cardboard is putrefied. Tiny scavenger fish swarm into this under-water version of an all-you-can-eat buffet.

Where could Tisa have hidden it?

By Minute Three, I've moved into the two smaller cabins. No tube.

I swim into the stateroom. A family of octopi occupies the waterfall shower stall in the marble bathroom. The tube isn't in the bathroom's drawers or cabinets.

In the master cabin, the built-in king-size bed has handcuffs on the headboard and footboard. Having also had a run-in with Oskar, I'm not surprised.

The bed's top sheet is still tucked into the frame. Affected by the centrifugal force of currents, it rises and falls as if it's haunted.

An apparition floats by: a concierge's caftan. Since Tisa's body was naked when we found her, it must have belonged to her.

I am about to give up when, out of the corner of my eye, I see something glistening in the bedroom air vent:

The cigar tube.

I slide open its slats and inch the tube out—

When, suddenly, I feel a presence:

Emmanuel.

He's dressed in the clothes he'd put on—

Except for the John Lobbs. He'd never have worn them in the water.

Instead, he wears goggles and an oxygen tank. He carries an HK MP5SD, most likely modified to shoot CAV-X water-to-water cartridges.

In other words, I've nowhere to hide, and he knows it. Grinning, he aims and then pulls the trigger.

I dodge below the bed's footboard.

Projectiles whiz overhead.

I've made enough bubbles that I'm out of his line of sight, but it's only a matter of time before I'm back in it.

As the tube floats by, he grabs for it—

But I do, too.

As we struggle, I grab the hose to his tank, jerk it away—

And take a big breath of oxygen.

Angry and panicked, Emmanuel wrestles me for the hose—

But I kick him away: hard, in the gut, propelling him backward.

He lets go of his weapon. Like me, he's focused on the tube.

Just as I grab it, Emmanuel reaches my side—

But his eyes follow a floating apparition:

Tisa's caftan.

It moves toward him as if she's alive.

Mesmerized, Emmanuel freezes.

Not me. After I slip the GPS disk into his shirt pocket, I cuff his hand to the footboard and propel myself to the door, locking it behind me.

Thank you, Tisa.

And then I remember:

I've got minutes—perhaps only seconds—to get away from the missile's final destination.

25

Kickback

*ny act interfering with a public official's ability to make
unbiased decisions—or, for that matter, an employee's—is
considered a kickback.*

*And because a kickback is a form of compensation for an
improper service or as preferential treatment, it is considered bribery
and, therefore, illegal.*

*A kickback—coming from "the Corrupter"—can take the form
of gifts, credit, or cold hard cash to "the Receiver."*

A kickback may also be sex.

*An economic study of bribes paid with either money or sex
showed two interesting results: kickbacks paid with money gave the
Receiver the most bargaining power. However, sex used as a kickback gave the bargaining power to the Corrupter.*

Blackmail, anyone?

I kick furiously toward the water's surface, then swim to the shore as fast as possible. After scrambling topside, I run to the beach beyond the mouth of the lagoon.

I scan the black ocean. The sun has barely risen beyond the horizon. Few rays undulate in the dark churning sea, let alone penetrate the inky sky.

And then I see the missile. It looks like a shooting star falling to Earth.

But shooting stars don't level out just a few feet above the water. And they don't swerve to make sharp angles before entering narrow inlets, only to suddenly plunge downward.

When the missile hits the boat, the explosion is deafening.

Suddenly, its body of water is a fish-stocked fountain that shoots straight up, rising high over the trees and leaving a muddy hole in its wake. I'm close enough that the blast lifts me off my feet.

I land on my ass in the lapping wave of a low tide, several yards farther from where I stood.

Dazed, I force myself onto my feet.

I must get to Yulia.

I run up the path that leads to Emmanuel's cabana. With all the fallen trees and broken limbs left in the storm's wake, it's not an easy task. In one instance, as I attempt to climb over a tree, I trip and fall, landing hard on my hands and knees.

I am so damn tired.

And yet, I pick myself up. I have to know if Yulia is still alive.

I look up the hill where Emmanuel's office used to be. It's now just a two-story hole in the ground—proof that Yulia completed her mission.

I run past the ruins of the event cabana, averting my eyes from the carnage. Though relieved that Jack and Claudio survived, I wonder how long it will take until I'm rescued. Surely, now that the storm is over, Investigator Salum will sail over to see what havoc the terrorists wreaked.

And salvage the body parts that haven't been feasted upon by bugs and beasts.

Finally, I'm in front of Emmanuel's cabana.

No one guards it.

I run inside, shouting Yulia's name while hoping—and *praying*—for a response.

None.

Again, I call out her name.

No response.

I run to the bedroom, all the while bracing myself for the worst:

Seeing her dead.

Yulia hangs limp in her cuffs, head bowed and eyes closed. Her burn is blistered and caked in blood and puss.

Putting two fingers under her ear, I pray for a pulse.

She's alive.

I thank God for that.

One eye opens. She groans.

Emmanuel left the keys to the cuffs on his table of horrors. When all four are open, I beg, "Try to walk with me."

At first, she shakes her head. But then she nods.

I coax her onto her feet. Still, the journey into the living room is arduous. She holds onto me as if her life depended on it.

We both know it does.

Gently, I place her on the couch. Yulia curls up in a ball. "Water…" she whispers through parched lips.

I run to the sink and fill a glass. As I hold it to her lips, she drinks too greedily and ends up gagging and upchucking. When she finishes dry heaving, she motions for more.

I refill the glass. While she drinks, she whispers, "Thank you."

I laugh. "Don't thank me yet. We still have to get back to civilization."

"He called someone," Yulia insists. "I don't know how or with what. Perhaps… a satellite phone?"

I open the credenza—

No satellite phone.

However, there is a shortwave radio.

I pull it out and flick it on. "May Day, May Day! This is Donna…" I pause. My impulse is to add "Craig," but then I remember all the grief I put Jack through.

I wonder if he's relieved to be rid of me.

But I also remember he too was so willing to doubt my love;

To assume I love Lee.

Suddenly, I'm crying.

"Donna, please, *Cheri*!" Yulia's croaks. "Say anything! Someone may be listening!"

So, I do: "This is Donna Craig! I am alive, as is Yulia

Tarasova, and we are the only survivors of the cyclone that hit the resort island of Kisiwa Cha Paradiso, just off the coast of Tanzania. Please get in touch with my husband, Jack Craig of Hilldale, California, via Acme Industries. Tell him I love him and that I hope he can forgive me for doubting him—and I hope he's come to his senses about any doubts he's had about me. I could only love him if he hadn't figured it out. He should never doubt that—ever! He should also let our sweet, wonderful children know I love them too—"

"This is Petty Officer Seacrest of the USS Hershel Williams. Copy on your May Day, Donna Craig. We're sending a RHIB to pick you up."

"That would make you my new best friend, Officer Seacrest."

"Aw, shucks, ma'am! I'm honored. And, as for your husband, Jack, and I quote him: apology accepted."

So, Jack and Claudio made it to the sea base after all.

"Jack…is there with you?"

"Copy that, ma'am. Along with our former Commander-in-Chief, Lee Chiffray, they are toasting your survival."

But…

Really? That's all Jack has to say?

No. *Thank god you're alive,* or *I love you, and I miss you too…?*

No *I'm sorry I was such a fool to have doubted you too, especially since Lee and I are now best buds in our mutual commiseration over your loss…?*

Why, those sons of guns!

26

Due Diligence

In the financial world, "due diligence" refers to an audit or review that confirms a financial statement's details. This is usually done by the party entering a proposed transaction with another.

This specific term has been co-opted in other industries. For example, lawyers may suggest that clients initiate due diligence on all contracts by hiring professionals with analysis training in some specialty area. That way, they can point out issues that may (operative phrase here) cause future concerns.

Is this a necessary evil? Sadly yes.

And it'll cost you a helluva lot of money.

For example, due diligence on a house you've just put under contract will entail looking at the foundation, the roof, the lot lines, structural soundness, warped walls, windows, doors, and infestation (ants, bugs, termites, etc.).

You may also want assurances that it is not an indigenous burial ground or spooked by someone who refuses to pass on.

Was the property a garbage dump, a nuclear test site, or a murder site in a previous life?

A lot to think about, eh?

That's what due diligence is for.

And aspirin is for the results of your experts' due diligence.

Suggestion: have a large bottle handy. (Just be sure to read and follow the directions carefully…)

"Tell me," I ask Ryan, "when, and how, did you suspect Emmanuel as the lead terrorist?"

"After our call with Marcus Branham, he received another: from CIA Director Landingham, confirming that Zanzibar's Chief Criminal Investigator, Godfrey Salum, had requested your assistance," Ryan explains. "As an aside, Landingham also mentioned what he thought was an odd coincidence: one of his agency's assets, the divorce attorney Rufus Coulter, was also on his way to Kisiwa Cha Paradiso with a female client who he suspected wasn't there for a quickie divorce but to liaison on a terrorist op."

"Good for Rufus!" I reply. "What tipped him off?"

"The assets from her prenup agreement were to be deposited in a small Swiss bank known to launder Kremlin money—not just for oligarchs, but for Putin too," Ryan explains.

"Let me guess," Jack says. "Oskar Surbeck represented that bank."

"Move to the head of the class," Ryan replies. "Rufus's hunch was right. The CIA tried to call him back to let him know TRACFIN put electronic tracers on all funds transferred in and out. However, the cyclone kept Landingham's people from reaching him. And Yulia's handlers at TRACFIN couldn't reach her either to give her a heads-up that she was about to come face-to-face with her soon-to-be ex."

"The bank involved was the one Emmanuel worked for right after college," I point out. "He plotted out the scheme with Oskar Surbeck. Because Oskar's English had a British accent, the blind Spanish banker, Claudio, assumed he was from the UK."

"Emmanuel was the American Claudio heard on the plane," Jack reasons. "Sabine dropped into her true Slavic accent among her old friends."

I ask, "Is the FSB to be informed of Sabine's extracurricular activities?"

"You better believe it. The back-channeling has already begun," Ryan confirms. "She may have escaped Kisiwa Cha Paradiso, but it's doubtful she'll survive Putin's wrath. One jab with the nerve agent, Novichok, and her last appearance on the *Hot Housewives of Paris* will be as the corpse in a funeral episode."

"It would send the ratings through the roof," Jack declares.

"I don't doubt it," Ryan admits.

"By the way, Investigator Salum told me Tisa was Emmanuel's sister," I tell Ryan. "He also divulged that she was working undercover at his behest. Yulia verified this. She was there when Salum made that request. Who better than a concierge to slip into the cabanas in search of clues about those who might be terrorists? Tisa had mentioned to Yulia her suspicions about her brother and the man who eventually killed her: Oskar. When I sympathized with Emmanuel's loss of his sister and offered to seek out clues of the terrorists, he played into it."

"Emmanuel also saw it as an opportunity to make you and Jack complicit with the crime," Ryan explains. "You did his dirty work by delivering the electronic pads capturing the bankers' eye scans. He'd also hidden security cameras in all the guest cabanas. After erasing the video of the three Americans attempting to rape you, Emmanuel sent the portion of the video of you killing them to Acme and Marcus, along with the ones of you and Jack rummaging through all the bankers' rooms. In exchange, he wanted safe-haven passage for himself and his accomplices. Otherwise, he'd release the doctored videos of your involvement."

"Which is why he preferred to make us his prisoners than kill us—or Yulia, for that matter," Jack reasons. "He needed hostages to trade for his get-out-of-jail-free card."

"And yet, he had no problem with torture," Ryan points out. But then, softly, he adds: "Donna, I applaud you for your guerrilla tactics against Emmanuel's crew, especially against the one you called...what was it again?" Papers rustle on his end. "Oh yeah, 'Jolly Green Giant.'"

Jack nods. "Ryan is right. It was brilliant. Of course, had you waited another second before tossing the grenade, you might have died along with them."

"I owe it to those years in which Jeff was between

fathers and needed his mother to teach him how to throw a curve ball."

Jack shrugs off my soft jibe. He's yet to sit down one-on-one with me, though it's been a few hours since we left the Williams and went wheels-up in Lee's jet.

I feel as if my heart has shattered into tiny pieces.

To hide my pain, I ask, "How are the bankers regarding PTSD?"

"Right now, they're just elated to be alive," Ryan reports. "Still, their brush with death will inevitably have emotional repercussions. On the upside, it should have a few positive effects too. Already, the survivors are recommending policy changes for additional aid to emerging nations. Bank profits are high. Taking from that pot, perhaps in exchange for tax credits, is one way to go. For that alone, I'd say the Craigs have earned another shot at a real vacation," Ryan declares.

Jack frowns. With a sideways gaze at me, he mutters, "That may be a moot issue."

My heart pounds so hard that I'm dizzy.

Ryan groans. "Take the hint, Mr. and Mrs. Craig. It's time to kiss and make up. I'll let you two hash out the details." He rings off.

I sit down on the couch. Jack eases beside me.

Neither of us speaks.

So much for detente.

Weary, I close my eyes.

In truth, it's because I don't want him to see me cry.

27

Rate of Return

Also known as "RoR," an asset's rate of return is the net gain or loss of an investment over a specific time and is indicated as a percentage of the investment's initial cost.

When calculating the rate of return, you are determining the percentage change from the beginning of any given period until the end of it.

Investments are like boats in the ocean: their survival is predicated on how well they weather turbulence. Whether your relationship can be measured in days, months, or years, be prepared for some disappointment.

If you were to calculate the rate of return on your investment in a relationship, you'd probably do it the same way. Be it days, months, or years, you'd choose a period to analyze and compare it to the period before.

If it doesn't measure up to those of the past few cycles, perhaps it's time for a change.

However, if you're satisfied with what's happening—despite the ups and downs, the stops and starts, the petty annoyances or disappointments—

Hang in there.

Better yet, double down.

Trisha and Jeff greet Jack and me with hugs and kisses punctuated by demands to see what gifts we brought back with us.

Hearing the commotion, Mary and Evan come bounding into the kitchen. I'm shocked—and, admittedly, dismayed—that they've come home from Berkeley.

While they're just starting their lives as a devoted couple, Jack and I are breaking up.

The way Jack puts it—"What are you doing here?"—takes them by surprise, more his tone than words. Mary's disappointment erases her smile. No doubt the look on my face does little to reassure her because her concern is now etched on her brow.

Besides Nicky's coconut head, we've brought other presents too. One of Jeff's is a tee-shirt sporting the pronouncement HELLO, MY BEACHES, and Trisha has one that declares CALL ME ON MY SHELL. Mary and Evan get matching puma-shell necklaces. There are also oversized sunglasses for our two gals and aviators for our guys. Everyone gets beach towels. The boys' are adorned with sharks. The girls' proclaim WHAT HAPPENS ON THE BEACH STAYS AT THE BEACH.

And yet, we don't fool anyone. Even as they ooh and

ahhh and josh around with us and each other, our children trade puzzled glances.

Kids have built-in Geiger counters that record their parents' emotional seismic activity. Ours notice that Jack's and my smiles aren't relaxed but forced and that our glances never meet. Our emotional tango is out of step.

The telltale sign that something is off-kilter is that we keep our hands to ourselves. We don't give loving pats or covert kisses that incite the kids to mutter, "Yuck!"

I'm not surprised that, within a half hour, Mary and Evan state they must go to Evan's company, BlackTech, to pick something up.

"What, exactly?" I ask.

Like two Bambis caught in headlights, they freeze. "A critical report!" Mary exclaims, while Evan says, "My computer."

Jack's cynical guffaw has them running out the door with no further ado.

A beat later, Trisha nudges Jeff, who declares, "We've got to go, too. We promised to meet a friend—"

"I'll give you a lift!" Horrified that we said this in unison, Jack and I stare at each other, then at the kids.

Jeff and Trisha's eyes dart from Jack to me and then to each other. Their shrugs are nonchalant, but their responses are firm:

"That's okay, we'll walk," Trisha says.

"Yeah, coz…Trisha needs the exercise," Jeff adds.

If you could murder with a glare, Trisha's was a kill shot right between Jeff's eyes.

"Are you going to Janie's?" Jack's question is practically a snarl.

It has the needles on our children's built-in parent-o-meters leaping off the charts. Still, Trisha nods, then waits silently for Jack's response. She's wondering what possible objection he could have. She assumes none because she doesn't see the threat Jack envisions:

Against him.

And the life we've built together.

From Lee.

After they've gone, Jack mutters, "Make the call."

Ah…

Hell. "We can't just…talk this out?"

Jack adamantly shakes his head. "You don't understand. We've tried! For six years, we've talked in circles about this. About…trust. Or the lack of it."

He's right.

So I call.

Afterward, I tell him, "She can take us today."

Jack nods. "Let's get it over with."

The meeting or our marriage?

I'll soon find out.

"What I hear you saying, Jack, is that you feel Donna no longer loves you." Our marriage counselor, Ramona Locke, has used thirty minutes of the fifty-five allotted to this session to prod us into an honest discussion—

Sort of.

I mean, we haven't seen her in six years. How honest can we be?

The last time was only our second session with her. It took place immediately after Jack and my first mission together. I was so scared that the kids would be devastated when Acme reassigned him elsewhere that I did my best to alienate him first. At the time, I likened it to ripping off a bandage that was stubbornly clinging to my life's biggest gaping wound:

In my case, I'd already had one husband who'd deserted me and the kids: Carl.

And talk about timing! Carl did so on the day of Trisha's birth—

By pretending to kill himself.

He then joined the enemy: the Quorum, an international terrorist group.

Talk about the penultimate deadbeat dad.

I was scared stiff that Jack would be yet another spy who loved me and then left me along with my already heartbroken children.

How was I to know that Jack had not just fallen in love with me but with Mary, Jeff, and Trisha too?

At the time, Jack insisted that we meet with a marriage counselor to see if there was any chance of saving our newfound union. Now, he wants closure on the failed national emergency-conceived experiment that is us.

Those many years ago, Dr. Ramona knew us as Carl and Donna Stone.

Considering this is a last-ditch couples therapy

session, I see no need to break the news to her that almost everything we told her was a lie.

Certainly not right now, as Dr. Ramona assures us: "It's easy to say that, over the past six years, the love you feel for each other has been sorely tested by the stresses of your jobs." Suddenly, she glances down at her notes. "What was it you do again?"

"International banking," Jack says.

I use my fall-back fib: "I'm a stay-at-home mom."

"But…you've just said that you, too, work out of the home." Dr. Ramona's sideways gaze puts me on the spot.

"Oh, yes!… I, um… sell cosmetics… to… friends and neighbors."

"I see." Dr. Ramona's brow furrows. "And from what Jack has described, you've admitted you're attracted to one of your clients?"

"Yes!… No! What I mean is… yes, Lee is a client. But just because Jack says I'm attracted to Lee doesn't make it true!" I glare at Jack.

Jack sneers, taking my stammering in stride.

Dr. Ramona pats my hand. "This is a safe space, Donna. There is no need to hide your feelings for anyone, including Lee. The truth gives us the path forward."

"Go ahead, Donna, tell the doc: *you adore Lee.*"

I retort, "Don't you mean Lee adores me?"

Jack guffaws. "Sure, okay. Let's call it that. Whereas what you have with Lee may be—as you so innocently put it to Dr. Ramona, 'a cerebral relationship,' don't bull-shit me or her about your feelings too. It's a hell of a lot more than that. When Lee enters the room, you practically drool—"

"How dare you say that!"

"Sure, I 'dare' to say it—*because it's true!*" Jack declares. "It's why you're always finding reasons to go and visit Lee. You revel in knowing that Lee adores you. Admit it!"

"I'll admit I appreciate Lee's graciousness, attentiveness, kindness—"

"Then damn it—" Jack stands and stalks the room. When he finally stops, his eyes are glassy. His voice cracks as he murmurs, "*Marry him already!*"

"*Him?...*" Dr. Ramona frowns. "Not that it matters, but...Lee is a man?"

"Yes!" Jack and I say in unison.

It's like a lightbulb over Dr. Ramona's head has gone off. She scribbles down another note.

"I readily admit I appreciate Lee's adoration!" I declare. "And you know what else I admit? That I can't just turn off all emotions during sex—*like you,* Jack!"

Riveted, Dr. Ramona's eyes shift back and forth between us. "Jack, Donna feels you aren't being honest with her—at least not in bed."

"To hell I'm not!" he roars. "I'm my most honest when we're making love."

I turn to Dr. Ramona. "He's right. But he won't admit he uses Lee's infatuation with me as an excuse."

"An excuse for what?" she asks.

"To ease his conscience for him having to do the dirtiest part of his job."

"And...what is that?" she prods.

Before I can answer, Jack declares, "That's just it, Don! When we've made love, I never turn off my feelings—but you better believe I do *when I'm with my targets.*"

"I don't believe it!"

"That I feel nothing for them?" Jack is now in my face. "Is that what you're insinuating?"

"Targets?" Dr. Ramona is now perplexed. "You target women…for sex?"

"Sometimes," Jack admits. "But then, so does she." He points at me. "Target men, I mean."

Now Dr. Ramona is writing at a crippling pace.

I jab Jack's chest. "Admit it! You do feel something when you're with them. Otherwise, you couldn't…well… *You couldn't get it up*!"

"You are so wrong!" Jack rolls his eyes. "It's purely a physical thing! *No emotions are involved.*"

"Ha! As if! Sex is an *emotional* response—Science 101, sir."

"You're so wrong! It's mind over matter. It's just part of the *job*. It's called doing what's necessary to accomplish the mission." Jack's voice shakes. "You say that you also find that part of our job disgusting. But, hey, admit it: you love playing the femme fatale. You get off on turning men's heads when they see you enter a room. You give them that come-hither gaze. And when you lick your lips, you're sending an open invitation for them to sidle up to you, to flirt with you, to ask you to bed."

"You *both* pick up other lovers?" At this point, Dr. Ramona is too fascinated to write.

"Yes!" We yell at her. But then we quickly add, "No!…" And then: "It's…our jobs!"

"Ah, now I understand! You're *sex surrogates.*" Dr. Ramona nods sagely. "Rest assured, I'm an expert in the issues that—no pun intended—*arise* in your field. Not to speak out of school, but full disclosure: I have several clients in your line of work! They meet right here every Thursday evening at eight o'clock." She reaches over to her desk, picks up two cards, and hands one to each of us.

I stand now because I'm too angry at Jack for assuming I love Lee and for not understanding the depth of my love for him.

Because I can't speak, I cry.

My tears fall faster than I can brush them away. Instead, I pull a handful of Kleenex from the box on the coffee table and cry into them.

The only sound in the room is my sobs. My wails.

My wracking pain.

Instinctively, Jack strokes my hair.

When I put my head on his shoulder, he turns toward me and cradles me to his chest.

I know this is supposed to comfort me. Instead, I heave to relieve the ache of knowing this may end us.

Time stands still.

But I don't mind. Because when we leave here, we will part ways.

When we meet in the future, our actions toward each other will be awkward and then achingly painful.

Eventually, a dullness will set in.

Who were we kidding all these years?

Just ourselves.

As hard as I fought my dullness when being stroked

and kissed and fucked by the strangers who, by well-targeted design, were my lovers, Jack met that part of our missions as if it were a physical challenge. He expected me to marvel at his emotional abstinence. Well, too bad! No matter how they got there, the hundreds of notches on his proverbial belt speak for themselves.

They wanted to be conquered. He obliged. They were willing to submit. He dominated. While stroking their erogenous zones, he also stoked their desires. With slaps and tickles and naughty talk, Jack uncovered their deceptions against our country or stole their state secrets without them even knowing.

Okay, yeah, I'll admit it: I did the same. But for me, it's not just another day at the office.

It's the ultimate walk of shame.

This is why our relationship was doomed to fail from the start. Why did it take so long to realize this and walk away before one of us got hurt?

Me.

Him.

The children.

Oh my God! … *The children.* I can't even fathom how we'll explain our breakup to them. They will feel they have to choose between us.

I would never want that.

I'm a liar. Of course, I'd want them to be angry at him.

As of yet, Trisha hasn't picked up on Jack's animosity toward Lee. But it's only a matter of time. At that point, her loyalty to him will come between her and Janie, her dearest friend these past six years.

Will she admit it to him? Doubtful. Nor to me, let alone to herself.

And, inevitably, she'll resent Jack because of it.

Even if Jack doesn't insinuate Lee's feelings for me, Trisha will notice.

So will Jeff and Mary.

This begs the question: what if they hate me instead?

What if, like Jack, they don't understand that I don't see Lee as anything but a friend?

I appreciate Lee's kindness, strength of character, and sense of humor.

Yes, I know he adores me.

Still, nothing Lee does will coerce me to leave Jack for him.

Only Jack can push me out of his life.

Only he can end us.

As if reading my mind, Jack pulls away. His silence is a scrim of stoic resolve.

Even Dr. Ramona picks up on this. When she rises, it's not to proclaim the end of the hour or to congratulate us on our progress.

Yes, we have moved forward in our journey. But we've done so separately.

Even she knows this.

When I stand, Dr. Ramona embraces me in a tight hug.

Jack rises next. Fervently, she shakes his hand.

Sheepishly, he says, "Full disclosure: we aren't sex therapists."

Ramona nods resignedly. "A shame. The group would have learned a lot from you. Primarily, how to process their feelings.. And if necessary, to get out of the business entirely." Her gaze goes from Jack to me and back to him: "That is what you'll do…right?"

Great question.

And yet, neither of us answers her.

How ironic if we end up clinging to the one thing that kept getting in the way of our love for each other, and that may be the end of us as a family:

Our roles at Acme.

Ramona starts to say something, but then thinks twice about it—

Only to finally spit it out: "If you don't mind me asking, what *do* you two do for a living, anyway?"

Jack and I look at each other.

Hmmmm….

Finally, Jack says, "Seriously, don't ask. Because… Well, we'd have to kill you."

Her eyes go blank. You can feel the fear in the silence of the room—

Until Ramona snickers. And giggles.

We do the same.

In time, the laughter stops. Taking both our hands in hers, she exclaims, "Donna and Carl, please—keep the faith you have in each other."

It's wishful thinking on her part.

Still, the sentiment is appreciated.

28

Futures

utures are traded stocks or commodities—bought or sold—via a particular price and on a date specified sometime in the future.

But seriously, who knows what the future brings?

No one.

And there's the rub. Have you (as they say in the South) bought a pig in a poke, or are you (as they say in Charlie and the Chocolate Factory*) holding the golden ticket?*

Paul Cezanne said it best: "We live in a rainbow of chaos."

Embrace your rainbows.

Embrace the chaos.

The ride home is made in silence. The house is empty.

No surprise there.

However, a note from Jeff is on the kitchen counter:

Me and The Brat came by the house to pick up our computers so that we could do our homework at Janie's. Afterward, we'll have dinner there, and then Mr. Chiffray is screening that new Zendaya movie coming out next month! See U afterward.

xoxoxoxox Jeff

I show it to Jack. He frowns, then crumples it into a ball and tosses it, high, like a three-pointer, into the trash can.

Score.

Not.

I know what he's thinking—that he'll be the one cut out of their lives.

Their love of Janie assures that Lee has already won them over.

I'm angry with him.

No, I'm angry *at* him—because he has so little faith in our children's love of him.

At that moment, I feel his eyes on me:

Glaring.

Warily, I retort, "What?"

"Nothing." He walks away.

Bullshit.

I shove him from behind.

He trips, catches himself, and then turns to me—

To grab me by the shoulders—

And to kiss me—

Fiercely.

And yes, I kiss back, just as fiercely, just as hungrily—

Just as remorsefully.

He picks me up and carries me to our bed.

Our bed.

Oh, how I've missed our bed!

How I've missed our life.

This is the thing about make-up sex:

It isn't about the sex at all. It's a given that it's going to be *really hot, really good*—

No, really: GREAT.

Nothing shows remorse better than a deep, penetrating plunge—

Followed by the slow, steady grind of unbridled lust.

Soft, damp, incoherent whispers fuel our frenzy—

Bemoaning the pleasures we've missed;

Regretting lost opportunities to make precious memories instead of wasting hours, maybe days, and being sullen and angry.

We vow to make up for lost time, here and now, not with words but with bliss-filled kisses and gentle caresses.

With euphoria so raw and piercing to our core that we revel in the pain of our agony;

With the realization that, together, our love is the most tremendous force against all doubt.

We overcompensate for what we lost these past few days:

Serenity.

Trust.

Sleep.

We rejoice in the joy of our shared lives.

When the punch-drunk drowsiness of our lovemaking fades, we are shy again. We almost lost each other. The last thing we want to do is repeat that folly.

We gaze into each other's eyes now. In a mere second, all that has happened to us and between us since the first time we set eyes on each other flashes before me. I know this must also be true of Jack because he, like me, whispers, "Forgive me."

Surprised, in unison, we add, "For what?"

After a pause, Jack replies, "For having doubted you."

"I was just going to say the same thing, I admit.

Then we kiss.

And hold each other until we fall asleep.

In time, our cells ping simultaneously with texts from Trisha and Jeff:

Hey, do you mind picking us up from Janie's? That way we don't have to haul our school crap back down the hill.

"'School crap?' Jack sighs. "Boy, that just shows you what they think of their one shot at getting into a good college."

"I think it's more of a reflection of laziness."

Jack laughs.

I grab the car keys.

Jack's smile falters. "I want to go too."

"Of course," I hand the keys to him.

Jack kisses my forehead.

We hold hands as we walk out, like teenagers.

Like old married couples.

Like lovers who know firsthand that life is fleeting.

Jack's face hardens as we roll up the hill to Lion's Lair.

When we've driven beyond the guard houses flanking the estate's massive gates, Porter walks out of the mansion's front entrance and waves us over.

Jack parks in the closest parking space. He's out of the car in a flash but doesn't open my door. Is it because Porter beat him to the punch?

I hope that's the case.

After a kiss on the cheek, Porter says, "Good to see the Craigs back in civilization."

I click my heels three times. "There's no place like home! There's no place like home! There's no place like home!"

Porter chortles. Jack is still stone-faced.

Yikes.

"I swear to you, Craigs, I had the kids wrangled for you. But then the girls ran off to gossip, and I sent Jeff after them. Don't ask me how, but he ended up in the pool." Porter rolls his eyes. "His clothes should be out of the dryer in another fifteen minutes. He's in one of Lee's robes."

"Great," Jack mutters.

Double yikes. I can't think of anything Porter could have said that would have been worse.

Porter doesn't lose his grin. But when his eyes shift to

me, he winks. "No ocean breeze today. What say you come on in out of the heat?"

At the pace in which Jack follows, you'd think he was on his way to the guillotine.

I'm glad he didn't look up. Otherwise, he'd have seen Lee standing at the window.

He's looking down at me.

Porter puts us in Lee's study. When he leaves, he doesn't shut the door.

My guess is it's a tactical move. Should Jack run for it, no door would hold him anyway. Not even this one, though it's a safe room, as are all the others.

Seven minutes pass without a word from Jack. All that time, he's pretended to peruse every book on Lee's wall-length bookcase. I'm starting to panic. To prod Jack into remembering a few of our greatest hits, I ask, "With Ryan, you mentioned my brilliance for thinking on my feet, especially when face to face with Emmanuel. But… Well, my point is… Were you… just being nice?"

Jack scoffs. "Don't be silly. If you're fishing for compliments, think back on all the accolades I've expressed in the six years we've been together."

By his curtness, I doubt our marriage will last another six months, let alone another six years.

Darn it, here we go again.

"Is it too hard for you to think of any nice things you've previously said? Okay, look—forget I asked!" I turn so he doesn't see I'm shaking from my anger. Before

I stop myself, I add, "Instead, how about even a half-hearted apology for accusing me of loving Lee?"

"Sure, okay—if you apologize for accusing me of enjoying the most disgusting part of my job."

It's my turn to laugh. "Boo hoo hoo! I'll cry for you."

"I'm being serious, Donna. It's as disgusting to me as your honeypot role is to you." I wince at the pain in Jack's voice. "But you and I know your feelings for Lee are different. Otherwise... *Otherwise, you wouldn't have enjoyed Lee's kiss!*"

After all these years, after all we've been through—

He still thinks I'd choose Lee over him.

It now dawns on me why:

Because he once lost the love of his life to another man.

He lost his first wife, Valentina, to my first husband, Carl.

Both are now dead. And yet, they still haunt us.

Carl's faked death taught me how to hate. And it gave me the thirst to kill. I did so to avenge his supposed death.

As for Jack, Valentina's betrayal—with Carl—is why Jack can't trust me with Lee.

Suddenly, I get it:

The reason Jack thinks nothing of bedding other women, the reason that part of our job disgusts him as much as it disgusts me—is because he doesn't love them.

He loves me.

And because I have real feelings for Lee—and it's apparent that Lee cares so much for me too—my friendship with Lee threatens Jack's trust in me.

Just like every woman who Jack is assigned to fuck brings out the worst in me.

There's only one way to exorcise our ghosts: "Yes, okay," I reply. "Lee's kiss was a pleasant surprise."

"Finally! You admit you loved it!" Jack is so broken-hearted that his voice cracks.

"In truth, it wasn't so much that I *enjoyed* it than my relief that it wasn't a turn-off."

Jack frowns. "Come again?"

"You're not hearing me. I was concerned he was a lousy kisser. I don't know if guys get it. Let me make it clear. The wrong partner is always there for all the wrong reasons—especially when the person in question has money and power, which Lee has in abundance." I think for a moment. "Not to mention he's certainly easy on the eye."

"Let me get this straight: you think he's a decent kisser, and that he's handsome, and he's as wealthy as Croesus. If you're trying to save our marriage, you're failing miserably." Jack's tone couldn't be more menacing.

"Don't you get it?" I ask. "True love isn't about the size of your partner's bank account, social status. or celebrity. The right person doesn't just share an attraction or adoration. The right person comes along when you least expect it. It may not be obvious to either of you that you're right for each other. No matter. The rubber meets the road by how you, as a couple, handle whatever curveballs are thrown your way. The right person earns that trust every day of your lives *together.*" I take both his hands in mine. "Jack, I could never have that with Lee."

"Why not?"

"Because I already have my right person: *you.*"

"She's telling you the truth." Lee stands at the door. "May I come in?"

Jack pauses but then nods.

"I may be blinded by my love of your wife, but I'm not deaf. And to set the record straight, Donna is right: *I* kissed *her*—to her immediate and obvious dismay." He winces. "Truth be told, I'd venture to say she was…well, downright repulsed."

Jack expresses his disbelief with a grunt. But when his eyes shift my way, they shine with hope.

"I wouldn't put it *that* way…" I wink at Jack.

He turns away. I don't know if it's because he's trying hard not to laugh or because he's genuinely relieved.

Either way, we now know where we stand with each other, always and forever.

As does Lee. Over Jack's shoulder, he looks at us longingly.

Then, gently, he touches his hand to his mouth. The kiss he throws before walking out is his way of acknowledging my ultimate decision.

At least, I hope so. Even if he chooses to pine for me from afar, I won't be flattered, let alone encourage it. I've made it clear where he stands with me:

I love Jack.

And I will always be in love with Jack.

If Lee wishes to stay in my life—Jack's and my lives —he must accept this.

The thing about being "the one who got away" is just that: you didn't say yes for a reason.

I have the best reason of all:

I already share a love;

A romance;

A family.

A life.

With Jack.

If I have to spend the rest of it proving my love to him, so be it. Because, since the day he first saw me, he's done the same.

It's how relationships survive.

It's how they grow and thrive.

It's why we vowed, "Until death do we part."

Let's face it: for us, staying alive is the hardest part of keeping that bargain.

This begs the question: how long can we stay in this business?

"We need to talk," Jack says.

"Funny you should say that since I was about to suggest the same to you."

I'm smiling because I know whatever we decide will be the best for all of us.

When Jack leans in for a kiss, I know he feels this way, too.

THE END

Other Books by Josie Brown

The Extracurricular Series

Books 1, 2, and 3

The Totlandia Series

The Onesies - Book 1 (Fall)

The Onesies - Book 2 (Winter)

The Onesies - Book 3 (Spring)

The Onesies - Book 4 (Summer)

The Twosies - Book 5 (Fall)

The Twosies – Book 6 (Winter)

The Twosies - Book 7 (Spring)

The Twosies - Book 8 (Summer)

The True Hollywood Lies Series

Hollywood Hunk

Hollywood Whore

More Josie Brown Novels

The Candidate

Secret Lives of Husbands and Wives

The Baby Planner

How to Reach Josie

To write Josie, go to:
mailfromjosie@gmail.com

To find out more about Josie, or to get on her eLetter list
for book launch announcements, go to her website:
www.JosieBrown.com

You can also find her at:

www.AuthorProvocateur.com

twitter.com/JosieBrownCA

facebook.com/josiebrownauthor

pinterest.com/josiebrownca

instagram.com/josiebrownnovels